"I'm new. Just got in," came a husky whisper with a trace of an accent.

"You French?" the guard asked. "You don't sound like nobody in these parts."

"I can be anything you want me to be."

"Mac sent you?" The guard sounded dubious. "He don't cotton much to soiled doves, but they make so much money for him, he rents out his whole upstairs over at the Mountain of Gold."

"The saloon?"

Slocum frowned at the question. It was as if the woman didn't know who Mac was or that he ran the saloon.

"Where else?"

"Go on, get inside," the woman urged. Her voice slipped through the night like a soft, warm breeze. Slocum would have gotten excited if she had been speaking to him instead of the guard. As it was, he waited for some slip, some opening he could exploit to get away.

When it came, it came fast.

DON'T MISS THESE
ALL-ACTION WESTERN SERIES
FROM THE BERKLEY PUBLISHING GROUP

THE GUNSMITH by J. R. Roberts

Clint Adams was a legend among lawmen, outlaws, and ladies. They called him . . . the Gunsmith.

LONGARM by Tabor Evans

The popular long-running series about Deputy U.S. Marshal Custis Long—his life, his loves, his fight for justice.

SLOCUM by Jake Logan

Today's longest-running action Western. John Slocum rides a deadly trail of hot blood and cold steel.

BUSHWHACKERS by B. J. Lanagan

An action-packed series by the creators of Longarm! The rousing adventures of the most brutal gang of cutthroats ever assembled—Quantrill's Raiders.

DIAMONDBACK by Guy Brewer

Dex Yancey is Diamondback, a Southern gentleman turned con man when his brother cheats him out of the family fortune. Ladies love him. Gamblers hate him. But nobody pulls one over on Dex . . .

WILDGUN by Jack Hanson

The blazing adventures of mountain man Will Barlow—from the creators of Longarm!

TEXAS TRACKER by Tom Calhoun

J.T. Law: the most relentless—and dangerous—manhunter in all Texas. Where sheriffs and posses fail, he's the best man to bring in the most vicious outlaws—for a price.

JAKE LOGAN

SLOCUM AND THE BRITISH BULLY

J

JOVE BOOKS, NEW YORK

THE BERKLEY PUBLISHING GROUP
Published by the Penguin Group
Penguin Group (USA) Inc.
375 Hudson Street, New York, New York 10014, USA
Penguin Group (Canada), 90 Eglinton Avenue East, Suite 700, Toronto, Ontario M4P 2Y3, Canada
(a division of Pearson Penguin Canada Inc.)
Penguin Books Ltd., 80 Strand, London WC2R 0RL, England
Penguin Group Ireland, 25 St. Stephen's Green, Dublin 2, Ireland (a division of Penguin Books Ltd.)
Penguin Group (Australia), 250 Camberwell Road, Camberwell, Victoria 3124, Australia
(a division of Pearson Australia Group Pty. Ltd.)
Penguin Books India Pvt. Ltd., 11 Community Centre, Panchsheel Park, New Delhi—110 017, India
Penguin Group (NZ), 67 Apollo Drive, Rosedale, North Shore 0632, New Zealand
(a division of Pearson New Zealand Ltd.)
Penguin Books (South Africa) (Pty.) Ltd., 24 Sturdee Avenue, Rosebank, Johannesburg 2196,
South Africa

Penguin Books Ltd., Registered Offices: 80 Strand, London WC2R 0RL, England

This is a work of fiction. Names, characters, places, and incidents either are the product of the author's imagination or are used fictitiously, and any resemblance to actual persons, living or dead, business establishments, events, or locales is entirely coincidental.

SLOCUM AND THE BRITISH BULLY

A Jove Book / published by arrangement with the author

PRINTING HISTORY
Jove edition / May 2009

Copyright © 2009 by Penguin Group (USA) Inc.
Cover illustration by Sergio Giovine.

ISBN: 978-0-515-14590-8

JOVE®
Jove Books are published by The Berkley Publishing Group,
a division of Penguin Group (USA) Inc.
375 Hudson Street, New York, New York 10014.
JOVE® is a registered trademark of Penguin Group (USA) Inc.
The "J" design is a trademark of Penguin Group (USA) Inc.

PRINTED IN THE UNITED STATES OF AMERICA

10 9 8 7 6 5 4 3 2 1

1

A small pyramid of gold dust on the table in front of John Slocum mesmerized him. He held his cracked, stained cards close to his vest as he forced himself to tear his eyes from the gold and study the others playing poker with him in the Virginia City saloon. Two of the men he discounted right away. They were hard-rock miners out for a night of excitement. They were more interested in knocking back shots of the bitter trade whiskey and getting drunk than they were in winning.

For Slocum, winning meant surviving another few days. From the look of the fourth man at the table, he held similar beliefs. He drank as heavily as his friends, but something about him turned Slocum cautious. The whiskey took the edge off the aches and pains that grew hour by hour during a day's hard work in the mines, but this man didn't have the look of pain from work. Instead, his pain came from something more. When he coughed up a bloody gob and spat it on the floor, Slocum knew the man had consumption.

He gambled to feel alive for another few hours.

"You boys plannin' on walkin' outta here with my

money?" The man across from Slocum spoke to the miners, but stared hard at Slocum.

"Aw, Renfro, you know we like to win. We like to whore, too. And drink. All of 'em 'bout the same amount."

"Might be you'll fold early then," Renfro said, "and pursue your other interests, 'cuz I'm winnin' this here pot."

Slocum considered this nothing more than a ploy to steal the pot, but it worked on the two miners because they threw in their cards, took what pitiful few dollars they had remaining of their hard-earned money, and left. They laughed and joshed each other, and then found themselves soiled doves willing to let them fondle their breasts for a dime and maybe do a little more for not much more.

"Just you and me," Slocum said. "Of the three things you mentioned, winning is more important to me than women or booze."

"Pity 'cuz I'm gonna clean you out. Then I kin get myself both a whore and a bottle, but maybe not in that order."

"You have to win first," Slocum said.

"Your call," Renfro said. He hawked another gob in the direction of a cuspidor. His aim was perfect, undoubtedly from long practice. He put his cards facedown on the table and folded his hands atop them. Slocum thought this was a strange gesture.

"My raise," Slocum said. He used the edge of his cards to move the pile of gold dust into the center of the table. He kept moving chips and greenbacks until nothing remained in front of him. He had won small pots all evening, but that wasn't the way to get the money he needed to move on from the Nevada boomtown. Don't lose much on any hand and move all in for the big one had worked well for him in the past. It would now, too.

"That's a mighty bold bet," Renfro said. He rubbed his sleeve across his stained lips. "So's this." He pushed everything in front of him into the pot. "Reckon we're close enough to even that it don't matter, one way or the other."

"Close enough," Slocum agreed.

"Show 'em, mister."

Slocum flopped three aces onto the table.

"What do you have?"

"Not quite that," Renfro said. "Only three deuces." As Slocum reached for the pot, Renfro stopped him. "And a pair of sevens. I got a full house. Beats your aces, though they look mighty fine."

Slocum leaned back and watched his night's work disappear into Renfro's pockets. The man used the edge of a deuce to scrape up the gold dust and slide it into a small leather bag. Then he tucked away the chips and greenbacks in different pockets and grinned. For the first time Slocum saw the gold tooth in the front of the man's mouth.

"Take the rest o' my bottle. You look like you can use it more 'n I kin." Renfro laughed, coughed, and spat more blood.

Slocum reached over and flipped up the hands of the two miners who had left the table.

"How do you explain that?" Slocum asked. He pushed back from the table so he could draw the Colt Navy he had slung in a cross-draw holster.

"Explain what?"

"You showed a seven of clubs. There's a seven of clubs in the discard."

"What're you sayin'?"

"A deck's not supposed to have two of the same card in it, especially when one of those cards rested in a full house."

"I ain't no cheater." Renfro kicked back his chair and stood, then doubled over in a coughing fit. Slocum watched warily since the coughing might conceal a move toward a hideout pistol.

Renfro straightened and put both hands on the table to support himself. He looked at Slocum with hot eyes.

"I ain't no card cheat."

"Somebody put the spare seven into the deck, and it wasn't me." Slocum stood and squared off.

"Might be one of them miners. They ain't got the sense God gave a goose. Who'd go puttin' a low card like a seven into a deck to cheat? You'd put an ace or king."

"Not if you didn't want to arouse suspicion."

"I ain't givin' ya back any of the money. I won it fair and square."

Renfro looked past Slocum. This gave just enough warning for Slocum to drop his shoulder, half turn, and swing his fist in a short, sharp jab that ended in another bar patron's belly. The air rushed from the man's lungs and he collapsed, but by the time Slocum twisted back, Renfro had hightailed it.

"Don't go startin' no trouble, mister," called the barkeep. The mustached man rested a sawed-off shotgun on the bar to steady it. If he fired, Slocum would be cut in half, and would probably take one or two of the other customers with him to the Promised Land.

"He cheated me."

"Renfro's all right. He wouldn't cheat nobody," the barkeep declared. "Come on over and I'll give you a drink on the house."

Slocum considered going after the gambler who had waltzed away with his money. He didn't know for sure that Renfro had cheated, but it was likely. A less clever cardsharp would slide in a couple aces or kings, as Renfro said, but who would ever question deuces and sevens? The other two who had been in the game were nowhere to be seen, but they had lost most of their poke to Renfro, too. Or to Slocum and then to Renfro. If they had a beef, it would be with Slocum for nibbling away at their stake little by little.

Renfro had taken his chance and bitten off a mouthful.

"Keep your drink," Slocum said. "I got unfinished business to tend to."

His way was blocked by the saloon bouncer, who

glanced toward the barkeep for instructions. This instant of distraction was all it took for Slocum to draw and swing his six-shooter. The barrel landed alongside the bouncer's head, just above his ear. He groaned, reached for the gash Slocum had opened on his scalp, and then sank to the sawdust-covered floor, clutching his head and moaning.

Slocum stepped over him and into the cold night. The stark wind blowing from higher in the Sierra Nevadas chilled him. He turned up the collar on his coat and slowly looked around the town's main street as his eyes adjusted to the starlight. A few gaslights burned, but mostly the miners couldn't be bothered with such civic improvements. Across the street, a man and woman walked quickly, pressed together against the wind. Slocum continued hunting for Renfro, but saw no one likely to be the consumptive card cheat. He'd started to return to the saloon to consider other ways of making a few dollars when he heard a scuffle in the alley beside the saloon. The sound of a fist hitting flesh was too distinctive for him to ignore.

Another man's fight wasn't the right place for him to stick his nose, but he went to look, just in case.

A dark figure stood over a fallen man, beating him mercilessly.

"He's had enough. Let him be," Slocum said.

The attacker spun. The glint of starlight off blued steel gave Slocum an instant's warning. He went for his six-gun, drew, and fired at the same instant the night-shrouded man fired. Both missed, but Slocum dived for cover, rolled, and came up at the corner of an apothecary store next to the saloon as the other man fired again. Slocum poked his six-shooter around the corner and looked down the alley.

All he saw was the victim slumped on the ground. His attacker had fled.

Slocum stood and stepped into the street to get a better view of the alley. He jerked to the side when a dozen men boiled into the night from the saloon.

The barkeep swung his sawed-off shotgun all around and demanded, "What's the shootin' about?"

Before Slocum could explain, two of the saloon patrons went into the alley and rolled over the man on the ground so he flopped on his back.

"It's Renfro, Mac. That son of a bitch done gunned him down. And Renfro, he ain't even got a gun!"

"Been robbed?" the barkeep asked.

"Pockets are ripped off. Whatever he was carryin' is all gone."

"Gun down an unarmed man and steal his poker winnings," Mac said. "You're the lowest of the low. I—"

The barkeep lifted the shotgun with the intent of squeezing both triggers and emptying the deadly buckshot into Slocum.

"I didn't do a thing to that card cheat," Slocum said hotly. "Somebody was whaling away on him. I stopped him."

"Yeah, like we believe you're a Good Samaritan."

"And Renfro's attacker took a shot at me. I fired back."

"Renfro's got a bullet through the ticker, Mac. Shot at close range. Set fire to his vest and left a powerful lot of gunpowder all around the hole."

"You drop that six-gun, mister, or I swear, I'll do the town the favor of not havin' to pay fer a hangin'!"

Slocum saw that the barkeep wasn't backing down. He considered his chances, and they didn't look good. In fact, they looked downright terrible. Several of the men behind the barkeep were drawing their six-shooters. If he started shooting, he wouldn't get away alive. Chances were good he wouldn't hit more than the barkeep or one of the others in the crowd. The rest would have no trouble emptying their six-guns into him.

"I didn't shoot Renfro," Slocum said, dropping his Colt into its holster and holding up his hands to show he wasn't going to fight. "I'll get on out of here and let you figure who did that to him."

"I know who upped and killed my brother," Mac said. "I got my damn shotgun trained on him!"

This explained a lot, but knowing didn't help Slocum get out of this jam.

"Take him to the lockup. See if that worthless marshal of ours is sober enough to throw him in a cell."

"Uh, Mac, ain't you heard?" said a man at the barkeep's right side.

"Heard what?" snapped Mac.

"The marshal, well, he upped and left this mornin'. Said he was on the trail of a renegade Indian. That no-account deputy rode off, too. No one knows where he went. Point is, ain't got no official law in town."

"Then I say string 'im up. Here. Now!"

"We agreed 'bout lynchin's, Mac," pointed out the man who'd given the news about the absent marshal and his deputy. "No takin' the law into our own hands. We gotta try him. It's only fair."

"We try him, then we hang him. He killed my brother!"

"Come on, mister," said the man who had done most of the talking. "You're gonna need my services."

"How's that?" Slocum started to fight when a quick hand snatched away his six-shooter, but the sight of the twin bores on Mac's shotgun prevented him from doing anything about it.

"I'm the only other lawyer in this here town. You want a defense put up at your trial, you gotta hire me."

"The other lawyer's the prosecutor?"

"You might say that. He's my brother-in-law." The lawyer shook his head as they headed toward the end of town where the jailhouse stood dark and cold and lonely. "Never could see what my sister saw in him."

"How many times have you gotten your client off?" Slocum asked.

"There's no need to get into such things," the lawyer said hastily, telling Slocum more than he wanted to know.

Despite what the man thought about the prosecutor, his brother-in-law prevailed more often than not. Slocum wondered if he could switch lawyers.

"Inside," Mac said, herding Slocum at the end of the shotgun. Slocum staggered when the barkeep pushed him hard. He started to turn and swing, but his lawyer caught his arm.

"None of that. No reason to add to the charges they got agin' you."

"What's assault compared with being railroaded on a murder?" Slocum asked.

"Get in that cell," Mac said, grabbing Slocum by the collar and giving him a bum's rush. Slocum caught himself against the back wall of the cell and swung around, ready to fight, but it was too late. The cell door clanged ominously, followed by the *snick!* of a key turning in the heavy lock.

He grabbed the bars and shook. The building might be tumbledown, but the cell was sturdy.

"What are you going to do with me?" Slocum asked. He waited to see who answered. Two men exchanged uneasy looks and backed away, leaving only the barkeep.

Mac came over and truculently thrust out his chin. Before he could speak, Slocum moved like a snake. He got his hand through the closely spaced bars and caught the man by the throat. His strong fingers tried to squeeze the life out of the barkeep, but the man reared back, put his boot on the bars and kicked hard, prying himself loose from Slocum's death grip.

"You wanna know what we're gonna do with you? String you the hell up, that's what. At dawn. I don't give a good goddamn if you stand trial. You killed my brother."

"Where's the money I'm supposed to have stolen off him? Look. I don't have a dime on me. He cleaned me out in a crooked poker game."

"You hid the money."

"Where? Why'd I do a thing like that, if I'd just killed

him? I would have run. Somebody else robbed and killed your brother. I want that money as bad as you want Renfro's killer," Slocum said. He saw his argument fell on deaf ears. All Mac wanted was a necktie party with Slocum as the guest of honor.

"You're a tricky one," Mac said. He rubbed his bruised throat, glared at Slocum, and then left. Slocum heard him giving orders to a guard posted outside the jailhouse door. Nobody was supposed to come in until dawn, when they would have a noose tied and ready for Slocum's neck.

Slocum paced the tiny cell hunting for a way out. The jailhouse might be falling down, but the cell was secure. He rattled the door a few times, checking for any play that he might use to his advantage. The iron bars in the door were secure. The door was solid. The hinges were, too. He was caught like a bug in a spiderweb and was waiting for the hungry spider to return.

He used all his strength to pull at the bars in the window. He didn't even crack the plaster around the iron rods. He changed his tactics and tried to knock the bars out rather than pull them in. Neither way proved successful. When he had tuckered himself out, Slocum sank down on the thin straw-filled pallet. He couldn't sleep, and he sure as hell couldn't get free from the cell.

All he could do was wait for the inevitable.

2

In spite of his predicament, Slocum dozed, only to be awakened around two in the morning by a scuffle outside the jail. He sat up and rubbed sleep from his bloodshot eyes. It was pitch-dark inside the cell, but he caught the guard's silhouette as he opened the outer door with his back to Slocum. This would have been the perfect time to gun the man down, or grab him, or—

Slocum could do nothing as long as he was locked up in the cell. The door was more than ten feet away. No matter how he stretched or wished for rubber arms, it wasn't going to happen. He was at the guard's mercy. If the guard had any mercy, Slocum reluctantly thought.

Then he perked up. Someone else stood just beyond his line of sight and talked in a low voice with the guard. Slocum caught enough of the byplay to know that a whore had come to service the guard.

"You mean Mac done sent you? I ain't seen you in town before," the guard said.

"I'm new. Just got in," came a husky whisper with a trace of an accent.

10

"You French?" the guard asked. "You don't sound like nobody in these parts."

"I can be anything you want me to be."

"Mac sent you?" The guard sounded dubious. "He don't cotton much to soiled doves, but they make so much money for him, he rents out his whole upstairs over at the Mountain of Gold."

"The saloon?"

Slocum frowned at the question. It was as if the woman didn't know who Mac was or that he ran the saloon.

"Where else?"

"Go on, get inside," the woman urged. Her voice slipped through the night like a soft, warm breeze. Slocum would have gotten excited if she had been speaking to him instead of the guard. As it was, he waited for some slip, some opening he could exploit to get away.

When it came, it came fast.

The guard faced Slocum and started to warn him about making a fuss, then was falling facedown onto the jailhouse floor. The woman wore a cloak pulled around her shoulders, hiding her body. As she moved, she pulled it up like a hood to obscure her face. In her hand she held a length of iron rod she had used to hit the guard on the head.

"Where're the keys?"

"Hanging up on a hook on the wall," Slocum said in response to her question. He watched as she hunted around in the dark for what seemed an eternity before she found the key ring. As she stepped over the fallen guard, Slocum called out a warning.

Without breaking stride, she swung the iron rod again, hitting the guard alongside the head. He flopped back to the floor, more than stunned this time.

"Here," she said, tossing the keys to Slocum. He fumbled and almost dropped them. It took some time to find the right key and get the cell door open.

"Did you kill him?" Slocum pointed to the felled guard.

"I doubt it. He has a hard head."

Slocum grunted as he dragged the unconscious guard into the cell and locked him inside. Sure that the man wasn't going anywhere, Slocum searched the small office and found his Colt Navy in the top desk drawer. He checked its load, then turned to the woman to thank her. She had slipped outside. When he got out of the jail and looked around, she was nowhere to be seen. It took him a couple seconds to convince himself she wasn't a ghost. He inhaled deeply and caught just a whiff of lavender on the night air. That was hardly a fragrance favored by hard rock miners or bartenders intent on lynching.

He didn't waste an instant heading for the livery stable where he had left his horse. The mare snorted and pawed at the straw on the stall floor when she saw him.

"Quiet now," he said, soothing the horse. He didn't want to wake the stable owner, who slept at the rear in the tack room. Although he had paid in advance and wasn't running out on a debt, Slocum wanted to get away from Virginia City without a trace. No matter how mad Mac might be about his brother's death, he wouldn't be able to raise a posse if they had no idea where their prisoner had gone. From the main street in Virginia City, there were only three directions possible, but Slocum intended to make it as hard as possible to follow his tracks.

He could go north or south along the mountainside or west over the Sierra Nevadas. With the town perched on the side of the mountain like it was, going east would be foolhardy. It would take too long to make his way to the bottom of the hill, and then he would be visible for a day or more as he rode. He wanted to vanish into thin air, just as his unknown savior had.

Slocum led his horse from the stall and jumped into the saddle as he heard loud cries from down the street. The guard had been found locked up. Slocum didn't gallop off since that would draw unwanted attention, but he got off the main street, going downhill a couple blocks, and then cut to the north and found the road leading to the cemetery.

Virginia City was coming alive behind him, loud cries of rage rising like flames devouring dry kindling. Slocum knew it would be short-lived when they decided there was no way they could track him. The heat would die down and in a day or two, only cold, bitter ash would remain. Returning to Virginia City was not a good way to keep on living, he decided as he reached a fork in the road. To his right lay the town cemetery, and the left-hand route curled north and west into the mountains where he could lose himself.

As he urged his mare up a small slope, he straightened in the saddle and half turned. Slocum frowned when he realized he had been wrong about Mac not whipping up a posse. The thunder of hooves behind him warned of at least a dozen men coming after him.

Slocum considered his choices. If he went to ground, they would pass by and never see him in the dark. More than once he had tried to track at night and found how difficult it was. Even the best Blackfoot or Ute scout rode more on instinct than actual spoor. If the posse had brought lanterns, they might have a better chance finding fresh tracks in the rocky road, but Slocum saw no evidence of bobbing lights along the road.

He urged his horse down a slope and into a rocky ravine, hunting for a place to hide. It surprised him that they came after him, and even more that they had unerringly taken the same road he had. If Mac had sent men out along each road from Virginia City, most would come up empty and be pissed off at him, but Slocum cared nothing about what might happen to the barkeep in a day or two. Survival now mattered more than Mac's reputation at any time.

Slocum drew his pistol and waited tensely when he heard the approaching posse. They galloped along and then slowed at the spot where he had left the road. He wondered if somebody in the posse had second sight. There was no way they could have found his tracks. He would bet on that.

Slocum snorted as that thought came to him. He had bet on three aces and lost. It was time to stop betting and begin relying on his six-shooter.

"Where's the track?" The voice echoed down the slope to Slocum, grating and all too recognizable. The barkeep led the posse. Slocum raised his Colt and waited for the riders to come down after him. They would be at a disadvantage on the slope strewn with loose rocks. If he potshotted one or two, their horses would fall and create enough panic for him to finish off several of the men. That ought to be enough to send the rest running. They were miners and shopkeepers, not U.S. Cavalry used to combat.

"Over here. Got it, Mac. See it? Scrapes on the rock. Up above us."

Slocum relaxed. They were heading up the steep hill on the other side of the road. He considered how long he should remain there. Some of the posse might stay on the road. Alerting them would be deadly, but if he stayed where he was, they might spot him come daybreak. How long they would hunt futilely for him up into the hills wasn't something he could estimate. After all, he had been wrong about a posse even coming after him.

"There! I see 'im!"

Gunfire broke out. At first, only a few shots disturbed the still night, and then it sounded like Gettysburg being fought all over again. He grinned at the waste of ammunition. They were chasing ghosts.

"Damn, missed the horse. They got away."

The warning caused Slocum to perk up. The posse had flushed somebody, but it sure as hell wasn't him. Horses pawed the rocky road, and the men in the posse argued among themselves about what to do. Mac's voice cut through the chatter.

"Dammit, let's get up there and do what's right."

"What's right is fer us to be real cautious," came a pro-test. "He's got his six-gun. I ain't gettin' shot up fer nuthin'."

"I'll offer a fifty-dollar reward," the barkeep said. When nobody cheered him on, Mac said, "I'll make it a hundred and a month of free whiskey."

This got the posse on the trail.

If Slocum had any sense, he would have lain low and let them go off on their wild-goose chase—but he realized the only other person likely to be out riding at this time of night was his savior. He had no idea who the woman was or why she had clubbed the guard back in town, but he owed her.

Slocum led his horse back up the slope until he reached a spot just under the verge of the road. He drew his Win-chester from its saddle sheath and levered a round into the chamber. To his ears, the metallic click was louder than a gunshot, but the posse was too intent on finding their way up the side of the mountain to notice.

He sized up the situation, then shifted his aim to a rocky outcropping above them. In the dark he couldn't be sure of his target, but he didn't have to aim accurately. All he needed was a shot or two close to the base of the rock. He fired methodically, and every bullet hit where he intended—and produced the result he had hoped for. The heavy rock slipped under the onslaught of his slugs, and then cracked with a sound like glass shattering.

The posse let out a cry of fear as the miniature ava-lanche cascaded down the side of the hill. The heavy rock took two men with it. Another horse, without a rider, let out a squeal, more like a pig than a horse, and followed the posse members in the middle of the rock slide.

Slocum wasted no time. He slammed his rifle back into its sheath and swung into the saddle. He galloped north along the road, not waiting to see if anyone followed. The havoc he had created would keep the posse from seriously considering coming after him, no matter how much reward Mac offered for his head.

As he rode, he saw a dark shape moving parallel to the road and higher on the slope. His hand went to his Colt, but he relaxed when he caught a better sight of the rider. From the shapely curves, this wasn't one of the posse.

The woman finally got her horse onto the road and trotted alongside his.

"Good to see you again," Slocum said.

The woman was filthy and her clothing had been slashed to ribbons as if she had fallen into a patch of prickly pear cactus. Her dark hair streamed back from an oval face that glowed with an inner light in the reflected starlight. Even dirt and tatters could not hide the woman's beauty. She turned toward him and glared.

"What's good about it? You were supposed to ride off, not bring the posse down on my head."

"I saved you back there."

"You think that makes us even? I heard gunshots. Did you kill those blighters?"

For the first time, a British accent came through strongly. Her anger erased any attempt to sound American.

"I slowed them down, but they might come after us. Mac was pissed off enough to chew nails and spit tacks. That was his brother that died back in town, but you knew that."

"Why should I?" she asked primly.

"You saw fit to spring me from jail. You had to know why I was locked up. Or do you go around freeing desperadoes for the fun of it?"

"I know you did not kill that man. What you said to the barkeep was right. Where did the money go if you did kill him? There was no reason for you to hide the—what do you Yanks call it? The loot?"

"What part of England do you hail from?"

"It is obvious, isn't it?" For the first time, she smiled. "I try not to sound ever so British, but I am. In answer to your question, I am from Northumberland."

Slocum had no idea where that was. For all he knew it was on the moon.

"We need to rest our horses," he said.

"For the night?"

Slocum nodded. He didn't hear any pursuit, but Mac might have to wait until dawn before continuing his quest for revenge. Otherwise, none of his current posse would ride behind him.

"You riled them up a powerful lot," she said. Slocum stared at her, trying to figure out what she was getting at. "Killing in that town is an everyday occurrence."

"Not quite, but almost," Slocum said. He introduced himself, but the woman was slow in responding. "I just wanted to know who to thank." He touched the brim of his hat and said, "If you keep riding on the road, you can out-leg anybody on your trail."

"And if I cut across country?"

"They might see where you left the road. Drag some brush behind you a mile or so and that should confuse them. They're miners, not trackers." With that, Slocum put his heels to his mare. The horse put on a burst of speed. He had no intention of staying on the road himself, preferring to head across the mountains and get into California as quick as he could ride. He had nothing waiting for him there, but he knew what to expect if he stayed in Nevada. Since Renfro had been Mac's brother, the barkeep would never forget. Being in a position to ask anyone coming into the Mountain of Gold Saloon if they had seen Slocum would add to the man's reach and constantly fuel his need for revenge.

Slocum was better off as far from Virginia City as possible.

A few miles down the road, his horse began to tire. The flight had been long and hard and it was time to rest. Finding a game trail, Slocum rode up into the hills, hunting for a cave. It was still an hour until dawn, making his ride along the trail about perfect. Small animals would scurry along it soon, hiding any hoofprints left in the soft dirt. He doubted Mac would pursue. The posse had been disheartened and would prefer a shot of whiskey to getting shot at, but he had seen blood feuds that lasted for decades and across generations. Killing a man's brother left a deep scar.

Slocum knew that all too well. His brother Robert had died during Pickett's Charge, and that had changed the way Slocum thought about Confederate tactics and generals. He reached up and pressed his fingers into a vest pocket, tracing the outline of the watch tucked there. That watch was his only legacy from a brother he had idolized. As good as Slocum was as a hunter, Robert had been better. He had been a better farmer, and probably had been a better soldier.

Memories ran deep. Hatred ran deeper.

When he reached a level area, Slocum turned and studied his back trail to be sure no one would catch him unawares. After several minutes, he decided the only thing stirring between him and road were early-rising rabbits. The first faint pink hint of dawn lit the eastern sky. It was time for him to grab some sleep.

He dismounted and led his horse to the sheer rock face rising from the level area. Following it around a few yards, he finally found a shallow cave. His mare nickered at the sight of some tempting grass growing nearby. Slocum hobbled the horse, took his gear, and went to the cave to make his camp. His belly rumbled, but sleep was more important than food at the moment. He spread out his blanket and used his saddle as a pillow.

Lying on his back, he stared east at the lightening sky. Coming to Nevada hadn't been a good idea, but he had made worse mistakes and lived to joke about them. His eyelids drooped and soon he slept, only to come awake just as the sun rose above the horizon. Slocum grabbed for his six-shooter and aimed it at the person silhouetted by the sun.

In spite of his careful ways, somebody had managed to sneak up on him as he slept.

3

"There's no call for that," came a soft voice. The touch of humor riding along with the words caused Slocum to sit up, lower his six-shooter, and squint to get a better look. The curves he saw outlined against the sun were memorable.

"You never did tell me your name," he said. "Now you come sneaking into my camp."

"My name's not what you want to know, is it?"

"How'd you track me?"

"You told me how to escape the posse. Since you were so kind to share your trick, I thought you might also be inclined to use it. I was right. I found a spot along the road where the grooves from a sagebrush ran parallel. If wind had blown it, they would not have run straight to that game trail. From there, I just followed the rabbits all the way here."

"You're mighty savvy for a city-bred girl," Slocum said.

"I told you I came from Northumberland. That is quite the forested area. Very bucolic."

"Do tell."

"And I still haven't told you my name." The woman

walked closer and shifted enough so Slocum wasn't peering into the sun so he could get a better look at her. He caught his breath. She had been mostly hidden in shadow the other times he had seen her. Back at the Virginia City jailhouse, all he had noticed was the iron rod in her hand used to club the guard. On the trail, she had stayed turned away from him.

Now the full light of day highlighted her tanned oval face and midnight dark hair. Blue eyes brighter than any spring flower stared at him with a boldness that he found refreshing. She was no shrinking violet, but he knew that already. Over a once-white blouse and denim skirt, she wore a canvas duster that almost dragged the ground.

"It's not mine," she said, slipping out of the duster and letting it drop to the ground.

"It's a man's," Slocum said.

"Yes." She stepped closer, her black leather riding boots flashing in the sunlight. There didn't seem to be a scrap or nick on the smooth, well-polished surfaces. Then Slocum wasn't paying much attention to boots because she was unfastening the tiny pearl buttons on her blouse to reveal breasts about as firm and high and perfect as he had ever seen. She never took her eyes off him, and it took all his willpower to keep from gawking like some young buck as she dropped her blouse atop the duster.

"Do you like what you see?"

"Can't tell," Slocum said. This startled her. She opened her mouth to say something, but no words came out. "I need to see more."

At this, the dark-haired beauty laughed. Her teeth were as white and perfect as her breasts. She licked her lips, the tip of her tongue making a slow circuit that set Slocum's pulse racing.

"How much more?" she asked.

"How much more is there to see?"

He found out. She reached down and worked at the fastener on her skirt. The denim dropped to the ground, leaving her clad only in frilly bloomers. Through the thin fabric, he saw the dark thatch between her thighs. She ran her hands down her hips and slowly skinned out of the underwear. With a quick kick, she stepped out, leaving her clad only in the calf-high riding boots.

"Well?" she asked.

"I was right. There was more to see. Plenty more." Slocum studied her trim body from boots to the top of her head and back. Her hips flared and her waist was slender, the perfect combination to make him even more uncomfortable as his erection grew in the tight prison of his jeans.

"Is that all you want to do? Just look? I can oblige, if so." She turned slowly, giving him a full view of her rounded ass and trim legs and jutting breasts. When she looked back in the direction she had come, she stopped and bent forward, giving him an even more exciting look. Bent over, she peered around at him. The wicked smile on her lips told him what more she wanted.

"I've got a question," Slocum said, standing. He shucked off his shirt and kicked free of his boots so he could strip off his jeans and let his stiffened organ enjoy a moment of morning sun.

"Abigail," she said. "Abigail Cheswick."

"That wasn't the question I wanted to ask," he said, moving forward to slide his hands around her hips and pull her back into the circle of his groin. His erection parted her fleshy ass cheeks and then dipped lower to stroke along her sex lips. He groaned as he ran back and forth a few times. She was ready for him. Her inner juices leaked out and slickened his organ.

"How I want you to make love to me?"

"That's not it either," Slocum said. He pulled her hips back and found the exact spot to enter her. They both cried out as he penetrated her and sank into her tightness.

"What *is* it then?" Abigail wiggled her rear end, and almost caused Slocum to lose control. She surrounded him like a warm velvet glove that got tighter by the instant as she tensed her inner muscles.

"Why'd you get me out of the jail?"

"Y-you needed help," she said, bending forward and leaning on her hands so she formed a sexy arch. She widened her stance to allow him better access from the rear, then began thrusting backward to take even more of his hardness inside.

Slocum held onto her hips to keep her from sinking forward. In this position, he was able to thrust and withdraw with sure, hard strokes. He closed his eyes and let the warmth of the rising sun bake his face and bare chest. He couldn't help comparing this to the carnal heat all around his manhood buried within her.

He shoved forward, paused, then drew back slowly. He wanted to keep doing this all day long, but she was simply too much for him. He reached around her with his arms and lifted her off the ground. Her feet flew up as she threw herself backward into him. He lost his balance and fell to the ground with Abigail atop him. Somehow, he managed to remain inside her the whole while.

She faced away from him as she straddled his legs. She began rising and falling faster, controlling the pace now. Slocum lay back and enjoyed the sight of her round white ass moving and the feel of her around him. Then she cried out and her hips went berserk. Seconds later, Slocum exploded as the white-hot tide rose within him and blasted forth. Abigail continued moving until he went limp within her. Then she twisted around and flopped down on top of him, her taut belly rubbing against his and her breasts moving slowly on his chest.

"That was incredible," she said, her eyes still a little glazed. "I can't remember it ever being so . . ."

"Intense?"

"Different," she said. Abigail kissed him suddenly, and

then pushed back to sit across his lap so she could stare down at him. "I'm glad I rescued you. It would have been a shame to miss this."

"I've heard a man gets a hard-on when he's hanged."

"That might be exciting for the man but not me, unless—" She grinned her wicked grin and then laughed. "It is ever so much fun teasing you."

He reached up and ran his fingers over her still-pulsating nipples. She pressed her hands onto his so he would not move them away. She shuddered, closed her eyes, and rocked gently back and forth. Suddenly, she pushed his hands away and stood.

"The posse might be along at anytime. I wouldn't want them to catch me with my knickers down."

Abigail bent over to pick up her bloomers, giving Slocum the chance to lightly slap her taut cheek. She yelped and straightened.

"How dare you!"

It was his turn to smile.

"The posse's not coming after us. They're coming after *me*. As long as you're here, you're in big trouble."

"Oh, I'd say the big trouble that was in *me* was quite fine, thank you." Abigail began dressing, giving Slocum the cue to dress also. He reluctantly got into his jeans and boots. It had been a long, tiring night, and he had not slept for more than an hour before she had appeared. In spite of his tiredness, he was willing to enjoy Abigail's charms a second time. He could sleep later, but he suspected his chances with her were evaporating as the sun rose in the sky.

He wasn't even sure why she had sought him out. He asked.

"No good reason other than curiosity. You didn't have to give me such sound advice when we got away from the posse, but you did."

"It was the least I could do to repay you for busting me

out of jail," he said. He hadn't gotten a satisfactory answer from her as to why she had risked her life for a complete stranger. Abigail did not seem the type to do anything on a whim. That thought turned him cautious with her.

"We should get away from those men," she said. "Hightail it, as you say out West."

"You've certainly got the tail for it," he remarked by way of compliment.

"And it was indeed high. Be that as it may," she said almost primly, buttoning her blouse and tucking in the tails under her skirt's waistband, "we should find sanctuary elsewhere."

"You have a place in mind, I take it?"

"Of course I do," she said. "If we return to the road, it will take only a day, but if we cut across the mountains, it might take . . . several."

"Over the mountains it is then," Slocum said. "But I'm all tuckered out, and my horse isn't likely to go far before collapsing under me. I doubt your horse is in better condition." He looked around and listened hard. Then he sniffed the cool morning breeze as he searched for any trace of her horse.

"I left the poor beast down the side of the mountain," she said. "I didn't want you flinging lead all about in an attempt to kill a pursuer from the posse."

"I don't fling lead all about," Slocum said.

She eyed the worn butt of his Colt Navy and nodded slowly. Without another word, she turned and hurried away, following the game path. Slocum went after her, more to take a look at the road some distance away. He doubted the posse would be after him at all, but he dared not take a chance at being caught.

It was a good thing he looked. In the distance toward Virginia City, he saw a fair-sized dust cloud showing somebody was traveling in his direction.

"Hurry up. We got company on the way," he called.

Slocum looked for her, but didn't see where she had gotten off to. Uneasily, he watched the approaching dust cloud until he made out the dim shapes of several men. He had hoped it might be a stagecoach, but he had asked about the stage in town and had been told it only showed up once a week or so. Heavy wagons rolled along the road carrying bullion, but these weren't guards for such a shipment. At this distance, he could not make out individual faces, but he knew he would recognize at least one if the riders got closer.

Mac was not going to give up.

"Abigail!" He slid his six-gun from its holster and started downhill to find her. It wouldn't be much longer before the posse reached a spot in the road where they could see anyone on the hillside and wonder who might be camped there.

He had gone only a dozen yards when he heard her muttering under her breath and found her tugging at a balky horse. The animal refused to budge, even when she yanked on the bridle.

"That's not going to get the horse up the hill," Slocum said. He slipped his pistol back in the holster, took the reins from her hand, and vaulted into the saddle. The horse tried to buck. Slocum rode out the first few attempts to unseat him. Then he applied his spurs to the horse's flanks. This caused it to rocket forward and come out on the flat in front of the shallow cave where Slocum had tried to sleep. When the horse tried to keep running, Slocum drew back on the reins and shifted his weight to the hindquarters, forcing the horse to rear. He fought for control for a few more seconds until the horse surrendered to his abilities. Slocum jumped to the ground and handed the reins to Abigail.

"You got yourself a right spirited animal," he said. "I'm surprised he didn't throw you a long time back."

"Oh, this sorry excuse for a horse has tried," she said.

"I wouldn't call the horse 'sorry,'" he said. "It's a powerful stallion, but you ought to ride something with less spirit that you can control."

"I rode you and you have quite a bit of spirit," she said.

Slocum laughed ruefully. She turned everything into a joke. "What are you doing out here? You don't have enough supplies to have ridden far."

"Shouldn't we ride farther into the mountains? To get out of sight of the posse?"

"You'll have to answer my questions eventually," he said. Slocum helped her mount and then saddled his own horse. They rode along the sheer rock face for a quarter mile, then turned into a canyon with towering walls on either side. Slocum didn't like the notion of having the posse trap him in a box canyon, but areas like this were favorites of the Indians. A few scouts along the rim, a box canyon, and a half dozen warriors behind made for an effective trap. Firing from above was easier than shooting from below, and they also had the ability to push down rocks. A small avalanche could take out an entire cavalry troop.

"This canyon opens on the other side of the range," she said.

He looked at her sharply and asked, "How do you know that?"

"This is the way I came on my way to Virginia City," Abigail said. "Retracing my path will take me directly to camp."

"Your camp?"

She only smiled, snapped the reins, and trotted ahead of him. Slocum became less worried about pursuit as he studied the ground. The trail they followed was hard-packed dirt and did not hold hoofprints well. In spite of this, he saw evidence that two riders had emerged from the canyon and one had ridden back. From what he could tell, the rider ahead of them had passed through less than a day before.

Slocum pieced together what he knew since Abigail wasn't up to telling him. She and another rider had gone into Virginia City and the other rider had left her there and retraced this trail. This was about as far as Slocum got because he began to doze in the saddle as the day wore on. The sun warmed the rock walls and turned the canyon into a furnace. If it had not been for a small trickle of a stream, he would have insisted they stop. As it was, a drink now and then and the gentle rocking of the mare under him lulled him to sleep.

"There," she said. "Ahead."

Slocum jerked awake. He reached for his six-shooter and then relaxed.

"Ahead, John, there's camp."

His keen eyes found the makeshift corral with a dozen horses in it. Four large, colorful canvas tents had been pitched, and flapped in the sluggish wind blowing through the canyon. Two men gathered together and pointed. Another emerged from a gaudy blue and gold tent and held what looked like a meat cleaver in his hand.

"Those are the servants," Abigail said. "Pay them no heed."

"Your servants?" Slocum was speaking to thin air. The woman galloped toward the camp, her long dark hair fluttering behind like a battle pennant. She drew rein and kicked up a cloud of dirt as her stallion dug in its heels. Then she dismounted. Without breaking stride, she handed the reins to one of the trio who had watched her approach.

Not sure what he was getting himself into, Slocum rode into the camp. The servants, all liveried, watched him suspiciously. No one offered to take his horse when he dismounted, so he tugged on the reins and kept the mare close.

Abigail had rushed to the largest tent and drawn back the flap. She called something he couldn't make out, but it brought forth a waspish man matching Slocum's six-foot height, wearing his jet black hair pulled back and fastened with a silver cord. He stood beside Abigail, waiting. Slocum had the impression of a cat waiting for a mouse.

"John, do come here. I want you to meet someone."

Slocum walked closer, aware of the man's dark eyes boring into him.

"This is William."

"William?"

"William Cheswick."

"Your husband?" Slocum sucked in his breath and wondered what was going to happen now.

"No, silly, he's my . . . brother."

Slocum felt a flood of relief at not having cuckolded the man, but he wondered at William Cheswick's reaction to the introduction. His face turned hard, and the eyes became cold chips of dark ice.

Slocum wondered what the hell he had gotten himself into.

4

"Pleased to meet you," Slocum said, sticking out his hand to shake. William Cheswick looked at the dirty hand and sneered a little before making a show of shaking. Then he made no attempt to hide his contempt when he snapped his fingers. A servant hurried over with a towel so Cheswick could wipe his hand clean.

"You are such a typical figure of the Colonies," Cheswick said. "Pleased to make your acquaintance."

Nothing in what the man said set well with Slocum. He reeked of some perfume, and looked as if he bathed several times a day. From the way the servants jumped at his slightest command, he probably ruled over them with an iron hand. In short, William Cheswick was everything Slocum hated. How he had ended up with such a lovely—and sexy—sister was one of the mysteries Slocum knew had no answer.

"Now that Abigail is safe, I'll be riding on," said Slocum.

"Oh, John, don't go. Not yet." She grabbed his arm and clung to him.

Slocum saw the surge of anger in her brother quickly hidden. It wouldn't take much for that anger to explode.

Perversely, Slocum wished it would. He had been falsely accused of murder, chased by a posse, and had built up a powerful lot of resentment. Punching Cheswick would go a ways toward relieving the tensions he felt, but the Britisher made no comment or move that would have let Slocum uncork a haymaker.

"Nothing for me here and plenty on my back trail," he reminded her.

"Tea," said Cheswick. "We're about to have tea. Quinton, prepare a tea. For three."

"Morning tea, sir?"

"What do you think, you idiot? Darjeeling! Must I do everything myself?" Cheswick made shooing motions that sent the servant scurrying off like a whipped dog.

"Now, join me in my tent. Why don't you, Mr. Slocum? And you also, my dear."

Slocum saw the look they gave one another, and realized a constant struggle for power went on between them. If anything, Abigail was more than capable of holding her own.

"Oh, brother dear, it would be *so* good to be in civilized company again." She held out her arm, but when her brother went to take it, she turned and denied it to him, presenting herself to Slocum instead.

It was dangerous getting between the siblings, but Slocum wanted to do something for Abigail—and to William. He let her loop her arm through his, and they walked briskly toward the large red, white, and blue tent, forcing her brother to run to catch up.

Slocum knew it was petty scoring such easy coup on the man, and he didn't much care at the moment. He was tired, hungry, and just a tad concerned about Mac and how long his posse would stay on the trail. Slocum doubted pursuit would last long. It might even have died off by now, with the miners needing to return to their lonely, dangerous jobs to make another dollar scrabbling out flecks of gold from the earth.

"My dear . . . sister. Sit beside me." Cheswick hurried around and held out a chair for Abigail. She bowed slightly and allowed him to seat her. Slocum dropped into a chair opposite Cheswick with a fancy inlaid wood table between them.

"You like this . . . trinket?" Cheswick asked, seeing Slocum's interest in the table. "It was a present from a maharajah in India, you know. He gave it to me because I bagged a man-eating tiger that positively decimated several of his villages."

"You're a hunter?"

"Oh, yes, William is a splendid hunter," Abigail cut in. "He goes on and on about it so much that it becomes tiresome."

"This is the West," Cheswick said sharply. "I'm sure Slocum would enjoy tales of my kills."

"*His* kills aren't animals. They're humans," Abigail said, her eyes going to the worn ebony handle on his Colt. Or was she looking at something else near where he slung his six-shooter? Slocum couldn't tell, but her cheeks showed roses now and her breasts rose and fell a little faster. Something excited her. Slocum hoped it was him rather than the idea that he had killed men.

"I'm sure," Cheswick said dryly. "Do tell me about yourself. You look . . . capable."

"Oh, he is, William. He's very capable."

Slocum caught the small twitch at the corner of Cheswick's mouth. Abigail's implication was clear.

"Yes, of course," said Cheswick. "As I was saying, traveling through your primitive countryside has been invigorating, but I am missing so much trying to find it myself."

"Find what?" Slocum asked.

"Why, my good man, adventure! It is positively *boring* back in merry old England. I came to the Colonies to get away from all the tedious riding to the hounds and those dreary cotillions that my . . . sister insists I attend."

"You enjoy flirting with the ladies, William," Abigail said. "I know you do, no matter how much you deny it."

"And you enjoy bringing home strays," he said harshly. As quick as a lightning bolt, his mood changed and he beckoned to a pair of servants in the tent door. "Come, come. Serve the tea. Be quick about it."

"Or he'll thrash you again," Abigail added.

Slocum couldn't tell if she was chiding her brother or warning the servants. The two men hurried back in and placed china cups and saucers in front of each of those seated, then hesitated, looking at Cheswick.

"Oh, get on with it. Pour." As the servants did, Cheswick asked Slocum, "Lemon? Cream?"

"I'll drink it neat," Slocum said. He felt clumsy picking up the delicate cup. He downed the contents in a single gulp. He preferred coffee so strong it ate its way through a tin cup. The tea had a faint taste, but nothing that appealed much to Slocum.

Cheswick laughed harshly and sneered. "My perfect barbarian."

"Prefer something stronger," Slocum said. He got to his feet and touched the brim of his hat in Abigail's direction. "I've got to ride on. Thanks for the tea."

As he reached the tent flap and pushed it open, Cheswick called out to him.

"Don't go, old chap. Do stay. I have a proposition for you."

"Your sister's already made one to me," Slocum said, enjoying the cruelty of the remark. Cheswick covered his reaction quickly by standing and hurrying to Slocum. If the Brit had tried to touch him, Slocum was ready to punch him in his smirking face and to hell with what Abigail thought.

"How much?"

"What's that?" Slocum stared into Cheswick's bottomless black eyes and read nothing there. It was like a whirlpool he had seen once that sucked in hapless men and devoured their bodies whole.

"I need a scout. A guide, you might say. You do know this country, don't you?"

"I have a passing acquaintance with it," Slocum said, choosing his words carefully. He wasn't sure what he was getting himself into with Cheswick's question.

"And the land within a hundred miles or so?"

Slocum nodded, not sure if he wanted to commit any further. Behind Cheswick, Abigail was still seated and watching the byplay with an amused smirk on her face. She took a sip of her tea, then held up the teacup in silent salute to Slocum. Her bright blue eyes twinkled and promised him paradise—if he stayed. Slocum wasn't sure he wanted that with her brother around.

"Five hundred," said Cheswick.

"What are you going on about?" Slocum asked, finally pushed to the limit of his toleration.

"I need a guide and scout. I'll pay you five hundred a month for that service."

"For how long?"

"A month, perhaps two, depending on how long it takes for me to find wild game sufficient to mount in the ancestral trophy hall back in England."

"That's all you want? That's a lot of money for something you can get from anyone else for fifty dollars."

"Dollars? I meant pounds. Five hundred pounds."

"Pounds of what?"

"Oh, John, William is offering you about fifteen hundred of your dollars to find him, what? A buffalo? A grizzling bear? Beaver?"

Her words slipped out silky and inviting. She put down her cup and saucer and leaned back in the chair, crossed her legs slowly, and sat like a man, one ankle perched on her other knee so Slocum could see her bloomers. It was even more blatant a bribe than what her brother offered.

"Is this your rifle?" Slocum scooped up a powerful double-barreled under-and-over rifle leaning against a chair.

"I shot an elephant in Africa with that," Cheswick said proudly. "It's a .610 Express Rifle."

"Powerful piece of hardware," Slocum said, lifting the heavy weapon to his shoulder. He paused as he sighted down the barrel, lowered the rifle, and then opened the breech. He looked up at Cheswick. "You shouldn't leave loaded weapons leaning against furniture. It's mighty easy for the rifle to fall over and discharge."

Slocum pulled the heavy cartridge from the top barrel and studied it. The brass cartridge gleamed in the light filtering into the tent from outside. The heavy lead slug had been scored to turn it into a dumdum. Slocum had seen similarly cut lead in weapons carried by soldiers who had served the British Raj in India.

"Guaranteed to bring down the heaviest predator," Cheswick said.

"Dangerous to keep around like this," Slocum said, closing the breech and putting the cartridge into his vest pocket. He hefted the rifle again. "You a good shot?"

"Oh, William's the best marksman I ever saw," Abigail chimed in.

"I always hit my target," the Brit said, giving his sister a look that Slocum couldn't interpret.

Getting involved with the Cheswicks would bring him a world of trouble. Slocum was sure of that. He might have passed up the offer except he had nothing but lint in his pocket. Renfro had cleaned him out back in Virginia City.

"Three aces," he muttered.

"Then you'll accept? Capital!" Cheswick slapped him on the back. "I'll see that you're properly outfitted, of course. Whatever gear you will need is yours."

"I got plenty. Some food for the trail is all I need," Slocum said.

"Better and better. I shall get my money's worth in no

time then," William Cheswick said. Louder, he called, "Quinton! See Mr. Slocum to the sleeping quarters."

"That's all right," Slocum said. "I prefer to camp under the stars."

"I must try that. It sounds so splendidly . . . primitive. But not tonight. Tonight, my dear sister and I have so much catching up to do."

Slocum and Abigail exchanged a quick look. She appeared irritated at her brother, but Slocum understood that. He had known the man only a few minutes, and wouldn't mind seeing one of the "grizzlings" he sought rip him apart.

"This way, sir," said Quinton, bowing deferentially as he held open the tent flap.

Slocum stepped into the bright afternoon sun, and paused for a moment to let the wind whistling down the canyon erase the sweat from his face. Sleeping in a tent, even a gaudy, extravagant one like Cheswick fancied, did not compare well with feeling the wind and sun against his skin.

"You will spread your bedroll someplace other than the servants' tent, sir?"

"Drop the 'sir,' " Slocum said. "I'm closer to being one of you than to him."

"My master is a demanding man," Quinton said.

"Your master." Slocum couldn't keep the contempt from his voice.

"He is quite generous, as you well know." Quinton sounded reproving without being too blatant about it. The servant led Slocum to a sandy spit behind the other two tents where the rude corral held the dozen or so horses.

"You've got some fine-looking horseflesh in there," said Slocum. "Only the best for him?"

"Absolutely, sir. In everything." Quinton looked apprehensive and then asked, "You did mean it when you said I didn't have to refer to you as 'sir,' didn't you?"

"The name's John Slocum. Any combination will do, and some folks add 'son of a bitch' to it."

"I'm sure they do, s—I'm sure they do, Slocum."

"Tell me about him. Your employer." Slocum wanted to ask more about Abigail, but didn't want to start too many rumors. All a woman had was her reputation, and besmirching it, even if she was a fancy English lady, would not do.

"He is next in line for the title of Duke of Northumberland. His brother Ralph was the duke, but he died unexpectedly. His next older brother, Percival, has inherited the title. Currently, Percival is roaming your country somewhere."

"That why William decided to come here? To ride with his brother?"

"His motives are much discussed, but none of us can really do more than speculate. One word of caution, Slocum. He turns viciously mean when he is in his cups."

"That's pretty often, isn't it?"

Quinton's expression gave all the answer he needed.

"Does he ever hit Abigail?"

"Oh, no, never. He knows better than that, even when he is, excuse the expression, drunk as a lord."

"So if he's not the duke of whatever, where's his money come from?" Slocum studied the horses in the makeshift corral. Whoever had chosen them had been experienced. There wasn't a plug in the bunch.

"He is a remittance man, having been given money by Lord Ralph to maintain his, uh, style of living."

"He was given money to stay out of his brother's hair," Slocum said.

"That is one way of looking at it." Quinton spoke in such a way that Slocum had to laugh. This was exactly the way the servant looked at it.

"Must be quite a pile of money to let him roam around with all this." Slocum made a pass with his hand indicating the tents, horses, and servants.

"Whoever holds the title is a very rich man. Very rich."

"I need a packhorse for later on. None of these will do. They're all saddle horses. What do you use?"

"A wagon. We keep the draft horses separate from these."

Slocum wondered how far that notion went in the camp, keeping the upper-class Cheswicks separate from the lowly servants. The way Abigail had jumped his bones, the practice might have only applied to the horses.

"From what I can tell, Cheswick wants some big-game animal. Would he be happy with a mountain lion?" Slocum asked.

"He bagged one of those already. It was duly skinned and stuffed and sent back to Northumberland for display. The duke was quite the hunter himself, and his youngest brother desperately wanted his approval."

"A grizzly bear then," Slocum decided. He would as soon leave the ferocious beasts alone. Even when a man was armed and firing from a distance, it was difficult to bring one down. A male could outrun a human, outclimb a cat, and outfight an elk.

"You know best, sir," Quinton said, slipping back into his ingrained civility.

Slocum thought about Abigail and why he was staying with Cheswick's hunting expedition, and wondered if he *did* know best. He shrugged it off. He could endure a month, then would have quite a poke and be able to go anywhere he wanted. He set about getting supplies.

Although it was almost sundown when he finished stowing everything in his saddlebags that he would need for a week-long scout, he decided to ride out rather than remain in camp. More than once as he packed, he had seen Cheswick studying him intently. The Brit always turned away when Slocum stared back, but the intent was obvious. Cheswick was sizing him up. Of Abigail, there hadn't been a trace. Slocum considered finding her to bid her good-bye before he hit the trail, but Cheswick's attitude made that seem like it would cause more trouble than it was worth.

After all, Slocum would be away from the camp and

Abigail had to remain behind. He remembered Quinton's comment about how Cheswick would never hit Abigail, but that could change in a flash. Cheswick considered himself to be in a lawless country, and even in England was hardly bound by the laws because of his noble birth. That combination might make him capable of anything, including harming his sister during a fit of anger.

"Will you need anything else, Slocum?" Quinton looked up at him as he turned his horse's face deeper into the canyon.

"Keep the fires burning, Quinton. And don't let anything happen that's too serious."

"I, uh, understand."

Slocum realized he was placing too heavy a burden on a man whose entire life had been one of service and silent devotion. He rode off without another word, glad to let the twilight wrap dark fingers around him.

The rocks radiated heat for another hour after the sun sank below the canyon rim, and then it turned downright cold. Slocum wasn't sure how far to ride, but he wanted to get out of the confining rocky canyon and into more open country. The wind in his face promised pine forests and heavy vegetation ahead. The canyon floor slanted upward and then became quite a climb. An hour after leaving Cheswick's camp, Slocum rode out into a broad valley that stretched into the night.

On both sides grew the pine and juniper he had scented earlier. From the nip in the air, he was within a thousand feet of the timberline, though the mountains were hidden by the darkness. This was a perfect place to begin his hunt for a grizzly's den. He planned to track it and mark the den, then fetch Cheswick so the man could stand off a ways and shoot it. Slocum didn't much like this, but he figured if all Cheswick wanted was the skin, claws, and head, there would be some good eating.

And facing the truth of it, when Cheswick bagged his

trophy, there might not be any reason to keep Slocum in his employment. Slocum worked over what he would ask for, and finally decided it would take a week to find the bear and get Cheswick back to shoot it. He would ask for two weeks' salary. That'd be fair.

Drawing rein, he stood in the stirrups and slowly studied the land. It would be better seen in daylight, but he wanted a feel for the terrain in both daylight and under starlight. Slowly turning, he took in the shape of the mountains all around, the tiny sounds and pungent odors that were the epitome of freedom for him.

Slocum stopped his reconnaissance suddenly. He couldn't put his finger on it, but something was out of place in this glade. Sinking back to the saddle, Slocum reached into his saddlebags and pulled out his field glasses. They worked better in daytime, but he wanted to catch motion rather than anything else. A careful circuit brought him to a dark figure moving at the far edge of the meadow, right at the edge of the trees. He focused the best he could.

A rider.

He watched as the rider stopped and almost vanished. The man faced in his direction now. Slocum caught his breath when a glint of starlight reflected. The other rider was using field glasses to spy on *him*.

Slocum lowered his binoculars and wondered what to do. As much as he hated to admit it, the other rider might be a lawman out hunting for him. If Mac couldn't nab him, he would certainly tell the marshal about Renfro's murder.

Slocum worked over his options, and finally came to a conclusion. He couldn't let the man report that he had found his fugitive—and if he wasn't a lawman, he was acting mighty strange.

He put his spurs to his mare's flanks and galloped off. If he wanted to get away, he had a powerful lot of work to do.

5

After several minutes of galloping, Slocum slowed to a walk, and finally let the mare rest a mite while he swung his field glasses around to see if he had been observed during his ride. He had. The distant spy had turned and still faced him. From the way the shadows played about the other rider, Slocum couldn't tell if he had trained binoculars on him, too, but he reckoned that he had. His short ride had kicked up some dust, but not much. It settled rapidly in the breeze whipping down off the mountains so the other rider had to have been watching through glasses.

Slocum angled toward the far side of the valley and wondered how long it would be until the other rider came after him. If the man was a deputy, he would come fast. How a lawman had gotten so far from Virginia City without passing through the canyon was something Slocum would worry on later. It might be that there were other passes through these mountains that Slocum knew nothing about—and the lawman did.

Cutting down into a ravine, Slocum doubled back using the bank to shield him from prying eyes. When he was sure

41

he had gone far enough that he wouldn't draw unwanted attention with a quick peek, he chanced a look to see what the mysterious rider was doing.

Slocum found himself caught in the jaws of a dilemma. The rider had disappeared. Had he come after Slocum or simply ridden on, minding his own business? Being jumpy at even distant travelers was unusual for Slocum, but he had to admit he had gotten himself into a real fix over in Virginia City. Someone had murdered Renfro, and it hadn't been him. That didn't matter to Mac, who by now might have set every peace officer in Nevada on his trail.

"And I had three damned aces," Slocum grumbled. How he could have lost with that hand was a mystery, but he was sure Renfro had slipped in the spare card to make that full house. He might not have seen him do it, but Renfro had cheated.

That he had cheated Slocum only gave others in Virginia City motive. How many had he swindled with his quick deals and sly palming of cards?

Slocum snapped back to the here and now when he heard the weight of a horse grinding down on gravel in the ravine he had just traversed. He drew his six-shooter and waited. He was a patient man, but the rider never showed himself.

Looking around convinced Slocum the horseman had gone up the far bank and was coming in for a clean shot— or maybe just to get a better look. They were playing a deadly game of cat and mouse, neither knowing for sure who the other was.

Slocum could have headed straight back to Cheswick's camp, but he didn't want to lead the law there. Abigail had sprung him from jail. Unless he found out otherwise, he had to believe the law was after her also.

Walking his mare along the ravine finally brought him to a spot where water erosion had cut away the bank. Slocum urged his horse up it, in a flurry of flying stones and far too much noise. If he had guessed right, he and the rider were on opposite sides of the ravine. This gave him a bit of a head start. Slocum galloped toward the wooded area on the far side of the valley, heading directly for the spot where he had first noticed the other man.

By the time he reached the edge of the pines, his mare was lathered and breathing like a blacksmith's bellows. He dropped off to rest her as he studied the ground for prints. It took the better part of a half hour, but he found the spot from which the other man had watched. The back trail led from the woods and then across the valley to the ravine. Slocum took no satisfaction in having reconstructed the man's trail because he didn't know where the man was at that instant.

He walked into the woods a ways until the hoofprints disappeared in the dark on the soft carpet of fallen pine needles. If he kept going in this direction, he could find where the rider had come from. He might also find a posse waiting with a freshly tied noose for him.

Indecision wasn't something that usually tormented him. It did now. He had come on a scout to find a grizzly for Cheswick to kill, and had found someone who might be a damned sight more dangerous. Tangling with the stranger wasn't going to help him much. If the man was a lawman, others would follow when he didn't return. And if Slocum did anything to a man who was innocent of anything other than being on the same range, his conscience would gnaw away at him.

He returned to his rested horse and began laying a trail so plain a blind man could follow it in the dark. He rode down into the valley, cut across it, and at sunrise waited to see if he had a tracker behind him. When he didn't see anyone, Slocum began doing all he could to make his trail disappear. Every trick he had ever learned or heard of being used by Apaches or Utes, he tried. By midday, he was tired, hungry, and sure that nobody this side of the Happy Hunting Grounds was going to follow him. They would follow and find his trail had disappeared like smoke in the wind.

It had been a lot of work, but Slocum thought it was worth it. He catnapped the rest of the day, did some quiet hunting, using only his knife to bag a rabbit, and then tentatively built a fire to cook it. More than once, he prowled about to see if anybody had spotted his fire—or his invisible trail.

He spent the night jumping at every sound, and when he awoke an hour before dawn, he was ready to return to Cheswick's camp and tell the man to move on. Coming in this direction would only get them all in trouble—or so it seemed to Slocum. Even if the rider hadn't been part of a posse, word of a reward got around fast in mining country. An eagle-eyed man could turn a quick profit by mentioning to a deputy who he had seen on the trail.

Slocum continued to do what he could to hide his trail, and eventually found himself in the mouth of the canyon leading back to Cheswick's camp. As he rode, an idea came to him how to collect some of that generous pay the Brit had offered without shouldering his way into trouble. There had to be other canyons and elevations where a bear might roam that weren't reached coming this way. He'd tell Cheswick he hadn't spotted any spoor and advise him to look elsewhere. If they traveled hard for three or four days, Slocum was sure they'd be far enough away from any possible posse to make a real bear hunt possible.

And safe.

All thoughts of safety evaporated when he heard the sound of gunfire from the direction of the camp. If Cheswick had been taking potshots at a target, there wouldn't be such sporadic firing. He definitely heard echoes from a gunfight where several different kinds of arms were being discharged.

Slocum looked behind him to be sure he wasn't caught between two halves of a posse, then rode into the camp.

The servants were nowhere to be seen, but the horses were still in the corral. He counted fast. One missing. Wherever Quinton and the rest had gone, it hadn't been on horseback.

"Abigail!" He listened hard for any sound the woman might make. Slocum hit the ground before his mare had come to a halt, and dashed into the gaudy tent where Cheswick slept. He poked around for a few seconds but found nothing. Going back out into the hot afternoon Nevada sun, he pulled down his hat to shield his eyes while he looked up at the canyon rim.

A cold knot formed in his belly when he saw silhouettes moving there. Those weren't lawmen come after him. Those were Indians. Canyons like this were a trap for the unwary, but Slocum hadn't heard about any recent uprisings. Then again, he had been more interested in poker and getting drunk while in Virginia City. The miners wouldn't fret much about Indians on the warpath because they spent their miserable lives underground clawing away at obdurate rock for the tiniest flakes of gold.

He hastily searched the rest of the tents and found nothing. Slocum turned slowly to study the scouts moving along the canyon rim a hundred feet above him. They all were heading away. When more gunfire sounded, the fleeting figures disappeared entirely.

He looked back down the canyon. He had ridden in from the lush, broad valley and had not spotted anybody. That meant the shooting came from the direction from which he and Abigail had approached the camp the previous day.

Sliding his rifle from the saddle sheath, Slocum set out on foot. His horse was too tired and nervous to be dependable. If he had to fire, he wanted something more stable than a crow-hopping horse under him.

Less than a quarter mile from the camp, he caught sight of movement in the rocks to one side of the canyon. Moving cautiously, he advanced. His Winchester came up, and he almost fired when a body surged forward and launched toward him. Only quick reflexes kept him from firing a round into Abigail Cheswick's trim body.

"John, oh, John!" She flung herself at him, arms circling his neck and almost strangling him. "It was terrible. H-he's hurt."

"Who is? Your brother?"

For a moment, she couldn't answer. She gulped and then nodded, keeping her head pressed against his shoulder. Slocum looked past her into the rocks but saw nothing.

"Where is he?"

"Back there. Higher up. They shot his horse. Out from under him. Then they attacked our camp."

"Indians?"

"They were red savages. William shot two of them and they rode away, but he was injured. They shot him with an arrow. I saw it st-sticking out of his b-back!"

"Stay here. I'll go find him. He's higher in these rocks?" Slocum waited until she nodded before he pushed her down and repeated, "Stay here. I'll be back in a few minutes."

"W-with William?"

Slocum made no promises. If the Paiutes had taken it into their heads to come back into western Nevada, there would be hell to pay. They had been pushed to the north, into Oregon, when Virginia City began drawing prospectors. The beginning of ranching and farming had further crowded them off their traditional land. It was nothing short of a miracle—or downright bad luck—if William Cheswick had run into a Paiute war party.

Slocum dodged from rock to rock as he moved higher. His caution was rewarded when a rifle bullet ricocheted off a boulder and sent chips flying into his face. If he had been less wary, he would have carried that lead in his chest. He dropped to his knees, sighted, and waited for movement. When it came, he fired and knew instantly that he had missed.

Not wanting to remain in one spot, he stayed low and circled toward the camp, then cut back sharply when he found a narrow crevice between two rocks. Squeezing through, he inched higher up the slope. Now and then, he looked along the rim for any sign that the Paiutes were gathering for another attack. They either were hiding better now, not outlining themselves against the bright blue sky, or had left.

Another shot rang out, indicating that they hadn't left. Slocum got a bead on the spot where the rifle had rested. When the flash of sunlight off steel barrel came again, he fired. His enemy's rifle went flying high into the air. The cry this produced startled Slocum.

"Blimey, I cannot believe any savage can shoot like that!"

"Cheswick?" Slocum kept his rifle trained on the spot, but now he began to seethe inside. "If that's you, Cheswick, show yourself now."

"I say, is that you, Slocum? However did you know to come help me deal with those barbarians?"

Slocum didn't budge. He waited for the other man to make a move. When he didn't, Slocum called out to him again.

"Are you injured?"

"Bloody right I am. An arrow in the back. They couldn't fight me face-to-face."

"I'm coming up. Don't shoot."

"How the hell can I? You shot the rifle from my hand."

Slocum made his way through the rock field, and rounded a boulder to see Cheswick leaning heavily against it. The fletched end of an arrow protruded from his back. He made feeble efforts to reach around and pull it out, but could not manage it.

"Let it be for the moment. If it didn't kill you outright, it's not going to do any more damage." Slocum had to be sure removing the arrow didn't cause a geyser of blood. He had seen men walk around for a day with an arrow in them, only to die when it got yanked free. Cheswick needed careful attention to be sure he didn't up and die.

"I've got my trophy after the dustup with those savages," Cheswick said proudly.

"That's quite a trophy, but I'll have to break it off to pull it free."

"Not the arrow, you dolt! Her!"

"What the hell?" Slocum thought he had seen it all, but William Cheswick had just trumped the stupidest thing Slocum had ever encountered. Trussed up nearby was a sullen squaw who glared at Slocum and then spat in Cheswick's direction.

"I captured her. I bagged her with a snare, like I would any wild animal."

"She's not an animal. That's a woman."

"They capture servants all the time in the African bush. I caught myself a new servant in the Wild West."

"You're out of your head," Slocum said. He wished he knew some Paiute to calm the squaw, but a quick look told him if he knew all the words in their entire language, nothing was going to get her to settle down. She strained so hard at her bonds that blood began to flow where the ropes cut into her flesh.

"I'll cut her free and—"

"You'll do no such thing. She's my prize. When she's properly trained, she will be the talk of all England. I know Sir Walter took heathens back with him while you were still a colony, and that created quite a stir, but those were braves."

"Not all of them," Slocum said. "Pocahontas went to London with her husband, John Rolfe. You thinking on marrying her?" Slocum looked at the furious woman, who was beginning to batter herself against the rocks.

"*Marry* her? That's rich," Cheswick said. "No, I think treating her as a servant will do quite well, thank you. Now, will you do something about this blasted arrow? It's beginning to burn like fire."

"You're lucky it wasn't a fire arrow," Slocum said, wishing it had been. If Cheswick had been killed, they might all get away with their scalps. Never in a hundred years could he imagine the Paiutes leaving one of their women behind as the prisoner of a white man. Women counted for little, but having them captured by enemies was a mark of utter shame. The Indians would do whatever they could to rescue her, and if they couldn't get her away, they would see that she was dead.

She would die, and so would Cheswick and Abigail and anyone else foolish enough to be around when the Indians attacked again.

"I need to get you back to camp before I pull the arrow out," Slocum said. If Cheswick agreed, they could leave the squaw behind to be rescued. This might be enough for Cheswick's party to leave the canyon without getting filled full of arrows and Indian bullets.

"Here and now. Take it out. I'm man enough for it."

"We need hot water and bandages."

"Abigail!" Cheswick snapped. "Tear off pieces of your petticoat for bandages for your dear brother's wound."

Slocum glanced over his shoulder, and saw a pale Abigail staring at her brother and the arrow jutting from his back.

"Listen to John. He knows about these things."

"Bosh. Do it." Cheswick turned ugly, a sneer on his aristocratic lips. "You might not have the stomach for it, but Slocum does."

Slocum was fed up with the man. He walked to Cheswick, placed his right hand against the man's back, and held him down so he could break the arrow off. Making no effort to be gentle, he spun him around, caught the arrow just behind the arrowhead, and drew it out fast. Cheswick sagged, then regained his balance. He had turned as pale as Abigail.

"That's the best you can do, I suppose," Cheswick said. He stumbled over, grabbed the squaw by the front of her deerskin jerkin, and pulled her to her feet. He shoved her ahead of him but kept one hand on her shoulder, as much to support himself as to keep her from running away.

Slocum watched them make their way down the hill. He caught Abigail's arm and held her back.

"Please, John. He's injured. I have to tend him."

"They'll kill us all because of that squaw," he said harshly.

"Her? But she doesn't look like anything, nothing at all."

"He kidnapped her. He has to let her go."

"Oh, William will when he tires of her."

A new chill ran up and down Slocum's spine. He worried what Abigail meant by that—and thought he knew. It was bad enough having a posse on his trail. Adding a Paiute war party would guarantee he never left Nevada alive. Not him, not anyone in the Cheswick party.

6

"You've got to talk to your brother," Slocum said. He tried to convince Abigail how dangerous it was keeping the Paiute woman in camp even overnight. If anything, if she wasn't freed to return to her own people immediately, night-time would become incredibly deadly. Slocum had heard too many tales of how the Paiutes could sneak up on a sentry who was both alert and warned and still kill him silently.

"Oh, William is such a bullheaded man," Abigail said, dismissing him with a wave of her hand. "What difference can it possibly make to the Indians? A woman more or less doesn't matter, does it? They treat them like slaves. William wants this one for a servant. She'll be treated ever so much better."

"She'll slit his damned throat the first chance she gets."

"Come now, John. You don't think he will allow her to have a knife, do you?"

"She'll rip his throat out with her fingernails. If her hands are tied, she'll chew his throat out and drink his blood."

"How melodramatic you are this evening." She looked

at him with her bright eyes and smiled. "You're trying to frighten me, aren't you? That's not necessary. You and I, well, we have an understanding, don't we? Ever since we escaped from the posse." She shivered although it wasn't cold. Slocum reckoned the nearness of death excited her.

"I'm trying to tell you what will happen if the squaw stays in camp much longer."

"But William is only now beginning to instruct her."

"If that means beating her, we might all be dead, no matter if she's released right away."

"He never strikes his servants. He has other ways of disciplining them."

"Starving her or tying her up aren't any better. She will starve herself to death if she has to."

"If she *has* to? That is ever so arch, John."

Slocum saw he wasn't getting anywhere with her. He had seen how her brother treated his English servants. Abigail might be right about him not hitting any of them, but Cheswick in his arrogance had a way of demanding to be obeyed that wouldn't set well with any Paiute.

He left her in the tent, and crossed the barren patch of earth between Abigail's tent and the huge red, white, and blue one. The evening breeze had died down and the flapping sounds earlier were now gone, so he could hear what went on inside. Slocum reached for his six-shooter, wondering if this would solve anything.

Before entering, he looked around for the other servants. He hadn't seen any of the trio since leaving to scout for the grizzly. They had either run off or been killed. Somehow, Slocum thought it might be better for them if they were all feathered with Paiute war arrows and being eaten by bugs and buzzards. It would save them from being tortured to death.

He went in, the canvas flap making a soft sighing noise behind him. William Cheswick looked up, a leer on his face that sent new chills through Slocum.

"What have you done now?" Then Slocum saw the Indian squaw tied to a tent pole, stripped to the waist.

"She is quite attractive, for being one of them," Cheswick said. He lounged back with a drink in his hand. For the first time Slocum saw Quinton standing toward the rear of the tent. The servant looked like Slocum felt inside.

"You're stark raving mad treating her like this," Slocum raged. "She has brothers and a father and maybe a husband. The Paiutes aren't known for being too friendly. You've assured us of an all-out attack because of the way you're treating her."

"She has nice bosoms," Cheswick said, as if he had not heard Slocum. "The chill of evening makes her nipples into hard little copper-colored pebbles."

Slocum stepped between the squaw and Cheswick and put his hand on his six-gun. He stopped when he saw that the Britisher held a derringer in the hand not clutching his drink.

"I would not like to kill you, Slocum, but I will if you attempt to thwart me."

"Thwart you? The Paiutes will *scalp* you!"

"They already did their worst and I survived." Cheswick raised himself from the pillows where he rested and moved his shoulder about. "Their arrow incapacitated me, but your quick attention made it all well again. Or mostly so. I still feel a twinge deep inside." Cheswick chuckled, as if he had made a joke.

"The only thing you'll feel inside is the cold steel of a knife blade slicing out your guts."

"You are overwrought. Did you find a bear for me to kill?" Cheswick peered at Slocum over the rim of his glass, which was filled with smoky-colored whiskey. It was so potent, Slocum could smell the liquor from across the tent. Cheswick might be drinking to ease the pain he had to feel from his wound, but Slocum doubted he was drunk. That made his behavior even more infuriating.

"No," Slocum said.

"A pity. It would be instructive to bag a grizzly, then have Little Flower skin it and prepare a meal in some traditional barbaric style. That would be quite the banquet, quite the celebration."

"Little Flower?"

"My name for her since she won't speak. In fact, all she does is spit at me, which is why I have her tied across the tent. No matter how she tries, she can't quite reach me with her next dollop of spittle." Cheswick held up his glass. Quinton hurried forward and handed his master another one already filled with Scotch whiskey.

"Your Indian name is Half Wit," Slocum said.

"You no longer amuse me, Slocum. Get out of the way. I want to study her aboriginal beauty some more."

"Look all you want but don't touch her. The Indians have a way of cutting off parts of anatomy that offend them."

"My, thank you for the warning. I am quite attached to most of my parts." Cheswick laughed as he scratched his balls. He lounged back and continued drinking, the derringer never straying from a spot dead center on Slocum's chest.

"I warned you."

"About nothing in particular," Cheswick said. "Go out and find a bear. Do that and I may forgive you."

"Yeah, I'll be holding my breath waiting for that." Slocum left, Quinton hurrying behind him. The servant reached out and caught Slocum's arm. He jerked free.

"Please, do not anger him. When he gets into one of these moods, he is likely to do terrible things."

"He already has," Slocum said, tilting his head to indicate the sorry spectacle inside the huge tent.

"He humiliates people. It is how he controls them," Quinton said.

"Where are the other two servants?"

Quinton's eyes grew big. He took a deep breath and said, "I don't know. They might have run off when the aborigines attacked."

"What the hell happened?"

"Lord William went out to hunt for grouse and came upon the Indian encampment. He saw, uh, Little Flower and took a fancy to her."

"A fancy," Slocum said, getting madder by the minute. He started back into the tent to settle accounts once and for all. Quinton moved quickly and interposed himself.

"He will get over it. He kidnapped her, and the Indians tracked him back to camp. They attacked. Burl and Charles fought well. They might have escaped. I don't know, but I helped Lady Abigail hide, and then lost track of Lord William. He must have slipped from camp with Little Flower and tried to hide."

"I know the rest," Slocum said in disgust.

"Don't do anything, Slocum," Quinton said. He rubbed his mouth with the back of his hand and looked frantic. "He has a temper. There's no telling what he might do if he takes it into his head."

"There's nothing he can do that'll compare with a mad Paiute warrior," Slocum said. He pushed past Quinton and walked into the twilight. He saw Abigail's shadow against the side of her tent, and turned to stare at the larger tent where Cheswick had his Indian captive. There was only one thing that could be done.

Slocum made sure his horse and another were saddled; then he hunkered down to wait. He dozed off several times, but when he came awake with a start, he knew it was time. Glancing at the stars told him it was past midnight. Cheswick would be asleep or passed out from so much whiskey. Slocum hoped he wasn't alongside the squaw in bed.

Quieter than a shadow moving along the ground, Slocum went to Cheswick's tent and pulled back the flap. A candle guttered on a table next to where Cheswick sprawled in a chair. His head lolled to the side, and he snored like a buzz saw. Slocum let the flap drop behind him to keep a vagrant air current from rousing the sleeping British lord.

He walked directly to the tent pole where the Paiute woman was still tied. She came alert and started to spit at him, but Slocum was quick and anticipated her move by forcing his hand over her mouth. He knew some Ute, and a bit more Navajo and Apache, but doubted speaking any of those languages would calm her. He also knew some Shoshone, but speaking that would infuriate her since the Shoshone were traditional enemies of her tribe.

Keeping his left hand over her mouth was a chore since she tried to bite him. He drew his knife. Her eyes went wide with fear, then narrowed as she prepared to die by his hand. He made two quick slashes that cut the ropes on her hands. She tried to hit him, but had been tied so long her hands lacked dexterity.

Slocum silently motioned with his knife for her to follow. Slowly releasing her and stepping away caused him a moment's anguish. She started directly for the sleeping William Cheswick, her fingers curled into claws. Slocum lifted his knife and poked her in the belly with the hilt. Hatred boiled in her dark eyes, and Slocum could not fault her for that. But he wanted her out of the camp as fast as possible. He poked her again, and herded her out of the tent into the cold night.

For a moment, she stood and stared up at the stars. The expression on her face was one of triumph. It quickly vanished and the anger returned.

"This way," Slocum said softly, figuring she knew enough English to understand. He hurried to where he had left his and another horse waiting. Only once did he have to stop and pull her along when she hesitated in the escape. He didn't have to speak her language to know her thoughts.

She wanted Cheswick dead. Slocum wondered why he didn't let her have her way with the Brit. Then he saw the shadow of Abigail moving inside her tent as she paced about restlessly. Why she couldn't sleep didn't matter. Slocum didn't want her to return to England after her brother was buried in some nameless Nevada pass.

"Mount up. The horse is yours. A gift," he said.

She swung into the saddle and glared down at him, but made no effort to ride away. A thousand worries flashed through Slocum's mind.

"I'll try to explain to your tribe what happened," he told her. He mounted and considered which direction to head. The Indians had been encountered back in the direction of the road leading to Virginia City, so he headed that way. The woman remained where she was, stolid and glaring at him.

"What more do you want me to do? I'm escorting you back to your family. Come on."

He walked his horse from camp, past Abigail's tent and farther, but did not get away without Quinton spotting him. The servant ran from his tent half-dressed and with a six-gun in his hand.

"Stop! I can't let you go. My master wouldn't like it."

"You ready to gun me down, Quinton? Go on and shoot me," Slocum said. He saw that fear of Cheswick and years of otherwise loyal service could not be overcome easily. Quinton lifted his six-shooter, and would have fired if Slocum hadn't acted first. He slid his boot from the stirrup and kicked hard, catching the servant under the chin with the toe. Quinton's head snapped back and he fell as stiff as a board, arms flung out and the pistol in the dirt beside him.

Slocum started to ride on, then wheeled about and galloped back in time to bend low and catch the squaw around the waist. She had dropped from her horse, intent on picking up the fallen pistol. He swung her around as she began to kick and claw until he reached her horse. Without slowing, he dropped her belly down over the saddle and caught up the horse's reins.

"Come on," he said, tugging on the reins to get the horse

moving. The Indian tried to slip off the saddle, but Slocum pressed her down until they were out of sight of Cheswick's camp. Only then did he straighten up. She slid feet first to the ground and started to run back to the camp.

"You've got a one-track mind, I'll give you that. But I can't let you kill that son of a bitch. I'm not sure why not, but I won't let you do it." Slocum considered doing the job himself, but Abigail kept intruding on his thoughts.

He slid the rope from the leather thong tying it to his saddle, made a loop, and then rode after the Paiute woman as if he was ready to rope a calf for branding. If anything, roping and hog-tying her was easier. The rope dropped around her body and down to her legs by the time Slocum yanked hard and looped the rope around the saddle horn.

He was on the ground almost as soon as she was, twisting and binding and finally having her trussed so she could only wiggle. She tried spitting at him, but her lip had been split in the scuffle.

"You're going back to your people—but without Cheswick's scalp." He hoisted her up over his shoulder, then put her back on her horse where he could lash her down like she was a sack of flour. "It's not a diamond hitch, but it'll do," he said as she struggled to flop one way or the other off her horse.

Slocum secured the reins to his saddle horn and started in search of the Paiute band. From the number he had seen high on the canyon rim, he thought there must be a dozen or more. If it had been a war party, women wouldn't accompany the warriors. That meant the small band was migrating, possibly to a higher elevation where the deer might be more abundant. The white men would be hunting constantly to supply the miners and other settlements in the area, leaving little for the Paiutes.

When he reached the mouth of the canyon, he looked down the road in the direction of Virginia City. He turned left and followed the road a ways, then spotted a small trail leading back in the direction he had ridden, only this small dirt track spiraled upward to the canyon rim.

"It won't be long before you're with your tribe again," Slocum told his unwilling companion. She let out a string of Paiute that had to be curses. If he hadn't worried she would beat him back to camp to kill Cheswick, he would have let her go here and now. Instead, he took the increasingly steep trail upward to the canyon rim. By the time he reached the edge, dawn again graced the sky with pale pinks and curiously curled grays of clouds building at the horizon.

They were in for a storm before midday, but he intended to get rid of his burden before then. What he did afterward wasn't as clear. He had agreed to Cheswick's offer of employment because of the tremendous amount of money offered for simple chores. Finding a grizzly in this country ought to be easy, but Slocum had other problems. As he thought of tracking a bear, he remembered the rider he had played hide-and-seek with in the distant valley. The man had been a mediocre enough trailsman, but Slocum wasn't going to bet his life that he had escaped detection. All his skills were dulled by fatigue now.

As he rode and peered down into the still-dark canyon, he realized that the money had been an excuse. He had appreciated what Abigail had done for him—and what they had done together after she had sprung him from jail. Putting up with her brother might be more than any woman was worth, though. He had to decide if there was any point in returning to work for Cheswick, even if only for a week or two longer.

"Whoa." Slocum dismounted and dropped to one knee. This was about the spot where he had seen Indians running along. He found footprints in the dust and more than one rock that had been kicked out of its earthen socket. The Paiutes had been running fast here, not caring if they left a trace behind. He judged distances and knew he was right. This was the spot.

"You're almost home," Slocum said as he stood. He considered riding, then decided it might be safer to lead his horse. By now, Cheswick would be awake and realize his new trinket was no longer in camp. Quinton might have recovered from the kick Slocum had dealt to his chin, but if he had, what would he tell his employer? The truth might get him fired or thrashed.

However that went, Cheswick would be storming around, still feeling the pain from the arrow in his back and furious. If he saw any rider along the rim, he might start shooting. Slocum wanted to sneak up on the Paiutes, then creep away after leaving the horse and its unwilling rider.

As he planned how to accomplish this, she began caterwauling.

"Be quiet," Slocum said. When he saw she had no intention of stopping her wild cries for help, he took off his bandanna and used it to gag her.

He continued walking, the rising sun at his back. Barely had he gone a hundred yards when he realized his caution had not extended far enough. Rather than worrying that Cheswick would spot him and open fire, he should have worried about the Paiutes finding him with their squaw bound and gagged.

Rising like a force of nature in front of him was a brave with a rifle aimed at him. Slocum glanced to his right and knew he was in big trouble. Two more braves decked out with war paint on their faces and torsos pointed their rifles at him. He didn't have to look to know a fourth stood behind him. He was boxed in on three sides by angry Paiutes, and the remaining side had a hundred-foot drop to the canyon floor.

Slocum raised his hands and hoped they didn't shoot him where he stood.

7

"I brought her back," Slocum said. He figured he was doing all right since the Paiutes didn't open up and fill him full of lead. "She belongs with your people." He started to lower his hands a mite, and that brought an instant response from the man directly in front of him. The warrior worked the lever on his rifle and sighted down the barrel. Slocum stared into a rifle bore that looked big enough to ride a horse down.

"Don't get itchy with your trigger finger," he said. From the style and color of the paint, he thought the warrior in front of him was the war chief. "I'm a friend. Here." He held out the reins to the horse where the woman kicked futilely and tried to scream around her gag.

Slocum plucked the bandanna from her mouth, and was almost knocked back a pace by the volume of her cries. She struggled against the ropes, but Slocum had worked the range too long to ever tie a knot that would come loose easily. He got to work on the ropes. If she had cooperated, he could have made short work of freeing her, but she kept up the verbal barrage and wouldn't stop fighting him, in spite of him working hard to release her. Finally done, Slocum stepped back a couple more paces and let the squaw flop onto the ground. She sat up, glared at him, then stood to face the man directly in front of them.

His guess had been right. The man she addressed had to be either her husband or the war chief—or both. The man let her tirade continue for what seemed all day, though Slocum doubted it lasted more than a minute. With a single word, the chief silenced her and motioned for her to get behind him.

"Here. Take the horse," Slocum said, holding out the reins. All the Indians had to do was shoot him and they'd get both horses, but this gave him a chance to step closer.

For a moment, the war chief lowered his rifle and started to reach for the reins. Slocum moved like a striking rattler. He lashed at the rifle barrel with the dangling reins, yanked, and moved fast to get behind the man. Slocum clamped his arm around the sinewy neck and tightened as hard as he could to choke the brave.

"Everybody stay back," Slocum warned. He had roped a tornado and didn't know what to do now. The rest of the band had him in their sights. War chiefs were voted on for each raid. While the man Slocum held might be popular, chances were good he had been voted out at some time in the past and another of the warriors had been chief. This presented an easy way to once more lead the war party for any of the others.

Kill their current chief and Slocum, claim the leadership again.

Attack came from an unexpected direction—or one that Slocum should have anticipated but hadn't. The squaw hit him from behind and knocked him forward. As he struggled to keep his balance, he found himself wrestling two tornadoes. The war chief fought furiously, and the squaw hammered at Slocum's back and head with her fists. She was strong, but the brave he clung to was stronger. Slocum's arm slipped and the Paiute warrior snaked away, hit the ground, rolled, and came up with his rifle in his hand.

Slocum straightened and drove his elbow back into the squaw's face. She let out a yelp of pain and staggered away, giving him an instant of breathing room. He stared at the brave holding the rifle and wondered why he hadn't fired. Then it hit him. None of the Indians had fired.

They were out of ammo.

A dozen things fell into place. They had attacked Cheswick with bow and arrow because they didn't have any cartridges. When they skulked along the canyon rim looking down, they had fired only a few rounds—probably the last of their ammo.

"I want to leave. No more fighting," Slocum said. He heard the squaw behind him making growling noises deep in her throat like some wild animal. The brave he faced tensed for an attack. The others advanced on him, hands going to knives sheathed at their deer hide belts.

Slocum drew and fired in a smooth motion, but his aim was off because he had a hundred-pound squaw dragging him down. He shrugged and threw her over his shoulder, but the rest of the band let out war whoops and came for him. He had no quarrel with them, but having his scalp lifted wasn't too enticing a prospect.

He fired until his Colt Navy came up empty. One Paiute lay dead on the ground and two more carried his lead in them, but not in any significant way to slow them. Slocum found himself bowled over by the nearest warrior. He hit the ground flat on his back, but managed to bring up his feet and drive them into the Indian's rock-hard belly enough to kick him away.

"I don't want to fight," Slocum repeated. He shoved his six-shooter into his holster and slid out the thick-bladed knife he sheathed in the top of his boot. The Paiute closest to him yammered something. Slocum was almost duped into listening. From the corner of his eye, he saw a blur as another attacked while the first distracted him.

He lowered his shoulder and caught the attacking brave in the center of his chest, knocking the wind from him. But Slocum knew this was a losing fight for him if he stayed any longer.

He kicked out, tangled the legs of the man in front of him, then recovered enough to vault over his fallen foe and run for his horse. The mare pawed nervously at the ground, as if preparing to attack. He vaulted into the saddle and let the horse rear. The mare's hooves raked the air in front of him and drove back two braves.

"Come on," he said, jerking the horse's head around. "Run like you mean it."

The horse shot away like a Fourth of July rocket. Slocum stayed low, caught the trail down, and followed the switchback—to his regret.

An Indian had run after him. Seeing him start down the winding trail, the Paiute waited, then jumped from higher up on the hillside. Strong arms tried to circle Slocum's neck and failed, but the man's heavy body smashed hard into the horse's flank and caused the mare to stumble. Slocum and the Indian went down in a heap, with the horse neighing wildly and kicking out as it tried to get back to its feet.

Slocum was momentarily dazed, and this was all it took for the rest of the war party to catch up. A strong hand seized his wrist and prevented him from pulling his knife again. Another fumbled for his six-gun, although it was empty. A pair of arms circled his legs and tackled him. Slocum realized that this attacker was the squaw. Whatever Cheswick had done to her had filled her with a fury not to be denied.

He punched and tried to get leverage to fight. The last thing he saw before day turned to eternal night was a jagged rock being raised high over his head.

* * *

Pain filling his skull and body, he blinked hard and thought he had gone blind. Everywhere he looked, he saw nothing but darkness. Then he smelled a small cooking fire and turned toward it. Heat from the tiny campfire warmed his face, and he saw the dancing, twisting sparks circling up into the nighttime sky. How long he had been knocked out hardly mattered as much as the way his hands and feet were securely bound with rawhide strips.

Twisting a little, hoping he hadn't alerted the Paiutes that he had regained consciousness, Slocum looked around the small camp. His heart sank when he saw two more cooking fires with dark, indistinct shapes huddled around them. He had been brought to their main camp.

He slumped back, working his wrists and feet around to see if there was any play in the rawhide bindings. There wasn't. He turned a little so he was looking across the nearest fire, and saw his six-shooter, gun belt, and knife hanging from a low branch of a piñon tree, too high for him to reach. Then he realized he had emptied his six-gun. Even if he got to it, he would have to take the time to reload. With so many in camp, he would be seen.

Gravel crunched behind him. Slocum closed his eyes and tried to relax because he knew what was coming. He bit his tongue to keep from calling out when a moccasined foot kicked him hard in the kidneys. A second kick, even harder, rattled his teeth, but he remained quiet. The Paiute guard wandered off, muttering to himself.

Slocum took the chance and swiveled about so he got a better look at the camp. He tried not to cry out in dismay. There had to be twenty Indians in camp, twice what he had expected. Getting free was a problem, but getting away would require a miracle.

"Three aces," Slocum muttered to himself. His luck had been running bad too long. It was time to change it. He rolled more onto his side to take the pressure off his right arm. No amount of self-control could have stopped his out-cry as sharp pain in his side made him wonder if he had rolled onto a knife blade. Rocking to and fro a couple times to get more comfortable only increased his puzzlement at what he was lying on. He lifted up a little and dropped down a few inches away and felt the same sudden jab.

Then he remembered putting Cheswick's large-caliber cartridge in his vest pocket when he agreed to hire on as a scout. Slocum's mind raced as he considered the possibilities. That single cartridge might be his ticket to freedom.

He had always shown great patience in his life. During the years he grew up back on Slocum's Stand in Calhoun County, Georgia, his brother Robert had cautioned him about rushing a shot or betraying his position to game wary of humans. Robert had always been a better hunter, and Slocum had learned well from him. During the war, he had been a sniper, content to sit in the fork of a tree all day if necessary to take a single shot. More than one battle had gone the way of the South because of his marksmanship—and patience.

But he was anxious to get the cartridge out where he could work on it. The only problem was the guard pacing back and forth, occasionally checking him to see if he had regained consciousness. As long as he could feign being out like a light, he had a chance. The Indians hadn't both-ered to gag him, which might be a help.

He repeated the single word to himself: patience.

The fires died down and the sounds of the Paiutes bed-ding down for the night buoyed his spirits. The guard might still watch him, but after several hours, he had to be nod-ding off. Slocum had not heard of any cavalry units in the area hunting Indians, and the only other menace the Paiutes might face was below in the canyon. William Cheswick was hardly a big obstacle, if they wanted to swoop down and scalp him and Quinton and take Abigail as a prisoner.

The Indians might not care, or the squaw Cheswick had

so foolishly kidnapped might harangue her husband or brother into attacking. Without ammunition, they had to rely on bow and arrow. If Cheswick saw them coming, unlimbered that huge gun of his, and accurately bagged a few before they got within bow range, he might drive them off. No matter how angry they might be at what he had done to one of their women, the Paiutes would not die to the last man to avenge her honor.

Another hour passed, and the fires were little more than coals now. Slocum had to act soon, if his scheme was to have any chance of working. Rubbing himself back and forth on the ground worked the huge cartridge from his vest pocket and left it on the ground. Wiggling like a worm, he managed to get the cartridge between his fingers.

Then came pain and tedium, and more than once the feeling that all was lost, as he twisted and turned and finally dislodged the slug from the rest of the cartridge. A significant reservoir of gunpowder was his for the taking now.

Moving slowly, he spun around and hunted for the guard. Not ten feet away the brave slumped forward, chin on his chest. He snored softly, testimony to his inattention to duty. Slocum grinned, and felt he had a chance for the first time since he had come to and found himself all trussed up like a Christmas goose.

He worked his way closer to the fire. The coals were still hot enough for what he had to do. When his wrists began to blister from the heat, he clumsily tipped the cartridge over and spilled the gunpowder on the rawhide strips. He winced as the powder sizzled against his skin as well as the rawhide. He jerked hard to break through.

The rawhide didn't break.

Slocum's heart hammered fiercely as he looked up and saw his guard coming out of his nap. The Indian sniffed the air and looked around. Slocum wasn't sure if it was the smell of the gunpowder or his charring flesh that brought the Paiute to complete wakefulness. Slocum slumped over and pretended to be unconscious. He got a foot in the gut this time that rolled him over into the coals. Try as he might he wasn't able to keep from crying out as the hot embers seared his back.

The Paiute growled and began pummeling him until Slocum almost blacked out again. He was dimly aware of being pulled to his feet and dragged along. He felt another rawhide strip being tied to him. This time it was around his throat. The other end was tossed over a limb above his head. If he slipped or passed out again, he would hang himself.

It seemed he couldn't avoid that no matter what he did. If the posse had caught him, they would have left him dangling from some tree limb. Now the Indians had done the same thing to him. He grunted as the guard punched him in the belly again, then gagged as the rawhide tightened around his throat.

Slocum blinked hard and got tears of pain out of his eyes. If he could have killed with a single look, the Paiute in front of him would have died a horrible death. The Indian grinned, acted as if he was going to punch Slocum, then lightly caressed his cheek. Laughing, the brave strutted off. Slocum pivoted enough to see that his guard had returned to his spot to sleep. Balancing precariously, he looked around. None of the others had come to see what the ruckus was about.

It was Slocum's turn to smile grimly. He still clutched the empty cartridge in his hand. He felt blood seeping from around the bonds holding his hands behind his back, but something more cut into his flesh. The edge of the brass cartridge was sharp.

Working methodically, trying not to drop his only hope of salvation, Slocum worked the edge back and forth. He cut himself as much as he did the rawhide, but when the strip suddenly parted, he lost his balance. He gulped hard as the rawhide sliced into his throat. Then he reached up and used the edge of the brass cartridge to slash at the strip. He tumbled to his knees. For a moment, he watched his guard, but the man was sound asleep again. It took another minute for Slocum to cut through the bonds on his feet, and another to rub circulation back into his hands and legs.

He tucked the elephant rifle cartridge back into his vest pocket for luck, then made his way carefully to the tree limb where his pistol and knife had been hung. He took another minute to load. The cartridges felt like sausages in his still-numb fingers, but he got the six-shooter loaded and strapped on the cross-draw holster before tucking his knife back into the top of his boot.

He looked at the sleeping guard, and considered a quick slash across an exposed throat as payment for the number of times he had been kicked and beaten. As strong as the temptation was, he faded back into the thin stand of trees, and made his way to the Indians' makeshift corral. Getting the hell away mattered more than ending a man's life, as satisfying as that would be.

Slocum saddled his mare and started to step up, only to find he couldn't. His belly convulsed in pain at the beating he had taken, and that bent him over almost double. When the muscle spasm passed, he tried again, only to find that his legs wouldn't bend enough to allow him to mount. He could try until the cows came home and get caught. Or he could walk his horse from the Indian camp.

One foot planted in front of the other, he made his way slowly away from the corral and away from the campsite. Or so he thought.

"Aieeee!"

The shriek of pure rage took him unawares. Slocum was slow reacting, but his horse reared and lashed out with vicious front hooves. The brave went down with his head stove in. Slocum stared at him and knew his luck was turning bad again. This was the brave who had been painted as a chief.

He tried again to mount, but his muscles still refused to obey. The noise had brought down even more bad luck on his head. He heard the shuffle of moccasins on pine needles, ducked, and missed a hard fist to his head by inches. He swung his elbow straight back and connected with an exposed belly.

"Can't I ever get away from you?" Slocum stared down at the squaw Cheswick had captured. She gasped for air, but the blinding hatred in her eyes told him that when she recovered she would come for him again.

Slocum drew his six-shooter and pointed it at her. This had no effect. She would die with all six bullets in her rather than let him escape. Not only was she taking revenge for what Cheswick had done to her, she wanted even more revenge on Slocum for killing her husband. Or the war chief might have been her brother or some other relative. It hardly mattered. Slocum had killed someone she loved.

As she stood and came for him again, he swung his pistol and buffaloed her. The barrel caught her on the left temple and knocked her to her knees again. Stunned, she went to all fours and shook her head. Slocum didn't dare shoot her. The gunshot would bring the entire camp down on his head, but letting her regain her senses was out of the question, too.

"Aw, hell," he muttered. He shoved her to the ground before she could get up and attack him again. Using his knife, he cut strips from her deerskin skirt. When she realized what he was doing, she cried out and began kicking. She probably thought he intended to rape her.

Stripping off his bandanna, Slocum shoved it into her mouth without getting bit. He finished cutting strips from her skirt, and lashed the crude bonds around her wrists. He tried to tie her ankles, too, but she was kicking too hard.

He grunted as he lifted her from the ground and dropped her belly down over his saddle. The mare protested the weight, but did not buck. Slocum held the squaw in place as he walked as fast as he could away from the Paiute camp. For an hour, he walked out the kinks in his belly and back and legs. Only then did he stop and pull her off the horse.

She landed with a thud on the ground, still trying to curse him around her gag.

"I need my bandanna back," he said. He caught one edge and yanked it free of her mouth. She snapped at him and missed. Slocum considered untying her, and knew that would only start the attacks over again. One of them would certainly die, and it wouldn't be him.

He pointed back along the trail he had followed. As he walked, he realized he was heading back along the canyon rim toward the broad valley rather than the trail he had taken to reach the summit.

"Go on, git," he said. She glared at him, then backed off and let out an ear-piercing scream. He considered gagging her again and forgetting about his bandanna, but he had paid damn near a dollar for that kerchief over in Denver and wasn't going to give it up. Slocum considered how far they were from the other Paiutes, and figured she could holler her head off and it wouldn't matter. Maybe the Indians would come for him when they found their chief dead. Maybe not.

He touched the brim of his hat in a mocking salute and took the reins in his hand. Somehow, the exercise had eased the bruised muscles, and her scream gave him impetus enough to vault into the saddle. His back hurt, and he wondered if he would be pissing blood from the beating. Probably. But as the mare trotted off in the dark, none of that mattered as much. Soon enough, he no longer heard the squaw. She had either shouted herself hoarse or had headed back toward her camp.

It didn't matter to Slocum. He was alive and in the saddle again and headed ... where? It was a decision he'd have to make quick.

8

Slocum wondered if there was a bone in his body that didn't ache or a muscle that hadn't been torn up as he rode. He tried nodding off in the saddle, but a new pain always brought him bolt upright. His mare found a trail down from the canyon rim into the grassy valley, and he looked over his shoulder just after dawn at the canyon mouth. Down that trail lay Cheswick and his camp. Or what remained of it. Slocum doubted the two servants had returned. Quinton was probably still with his employer, more out of habit than devotion. Cheswick could not be paying the man enough to put up with the guff that he did.

And Abigail was down there, too. Lovely, dark-haired, laughing Abigail. Slocum remembered the playful glint in her bright blue eyes and the way her bow-shaped lips curled into a smile. He remembered even more. The feel of her body moving against his would be pure pleasure now. His horse stumbled and almost fell, giving him quite a wrench. The pain convinced Slocum that the last thing in the world he needed was the demanding Abigail Cheswick beside him or on top of him or him on top of her. There are some things that a man just might not survive.

As pleasurable as it might be to die in her arms, Slocum had some living yet to do. He steered his horse away from the canyon mouth and cut directly across the valley, heading for a stand of trees. He intended to find a secure place to sleep for a day or two and recuperate. His earlier exploration, when he had played hide-and-seek with the solitary rider, had shown him where a stream ran through the meadow. Water, a bath, sleep. Those were the anodynes he needed most.

He zigzagged through the trees and came out into a small clearing. His hand moved to his holstered six-gun, and then he relaxed when he recognized the man in the clearing.

"Good morning, Slocum," Quinton said. "We had not expected to see you again after you left so suddenly last evening."

"I never expected to see you again at all," Slocum said.

"Lord William is out hunting for fresh game."

Slocum touched the elephant gun cartridge in his vest pocket and smiled just a little. If Cheswick used that rifle on a deer, there would be stew meat scattered all over the forest.

"How'd you get out of the canyon and out here so fast?"

"Lord William insisted we strike camp and get on the trail, as you Yanks say, immediately after discovering the aborigine gone."

"I'm not a Yank," Slocum said sharply. "Sorry. I've had quite a night."

"You appear to be the worse for wear," Quinton said. "Might I suggest a bath in the stream? There is a small pool that might be perfect for use as a bathtub."

"I could use some grub, too. You got anything to eat, or do you have to wait for your boss to get back?"

"He is your, uh, boss, as you say, also."

"Yeah," Slocum said. He started to dismount and found that he couldn't do it. "Could you help me?" He hated to ask Quinton for help, but it was the only way he could step down without falling heavily.

Quinton didn't say a word as he came, took the reins, and then eased Slocum to the ground. For a moment, Slocum's knees went weak, and he had to cling to his cantle to keep from falling.

"You are in need of medical attention," Quinton said, frowning. "Is there anything I can do?"

"Nothing wrong with me that a bath won't cure," Slocum said. He took a few steps and felt better for it. "That way?"

Quinton nodded. Slocum walked with increasing vigor and found the stream. It took him a few minutes walking upstream to find the catch basin Quinton had described as being a perfect bathtub. Slocum sank down on the rocky lip and began undressing. He found it hard getting his shirt off because of the pain in his back, but he finally tossed it to the ground. His gun belt and boots and jeans followed. Naked, he slid into the cold water.

He gasped as the frigid touch sucked the warmth from his body, but after a few seconds, he felt better. The cold was what he needed on his bruised body. Leaning back, he floated in the small pool and closed his eyes and just drifted.

A small sound caused him to thrash about and reach for his six-shooter. He stopped when he looked up at Abigail Cheswick. A broad grin stretched from ear to ear.

"I had heard there were all kinds of exotic wildlife in these woods. I never expected to find a naked . . . merman."

"It's good to see you, too."

"Ah, but I see ever so much more of you. Would you like company?" She began unbuttoning her crisp white linen blouse. Abigail stopped when she saw the expression on his face. "What's wrong, John? You don't like me anymore?"

"I can hardly move," he said. Slocum got his feet under him and stood. He turned slowly with the water lapping about his thighs.

"Oh, sweet Jesus," she whispered. "What happened? You're all covered with bruises. The big yellow and brown one on your back looks painful."

"It is," Slocum said. He sank back down into the cold water. The flow around him stole away some of the hurt. Some, but not enough for him to entertain the idea of Abigail frolicking naked alongside him in the pool.

"You took the Indian woman back to her tribe," Abigail said. "William was positive you had run off with her for some wild assignation."

"If you mean he thought the two of us were enjoying each other's company, I can tell you for certain sure neither of us enjoyed the other one little bit."

"I can only guess. They caught you? The rest of those savages?"

Slocum nodded. Even this small movement hurt.

"Let me. Come closer. I won't bite." She held out her hands to him, and then turned him around so she sat on the bank while he remained in the water. She began to massage the knotted muscles in his shoulders and neck. He winced as she touched the fiery line where the rawhide had been fastened around his neck.

"Whatever did they do to you?"

"They don't have any ammo left," Slocum said, not wanting to dwell on what had happened to him. "They must have run out when they attacked your camp. That's why they shot your brother with an arrow. They would have used a bullet if they'd had one left."

"I suppose William was lucky then, though it didn't seem so at the time." She continued to work out the tenseness from his shoulders, and then worked lower. Touching his ribs made him stand a little straighter. From the way she probed, he knew she was checking for broken ribs.

"I would have died on the trail if they'd broken anything."

"Good. I want you in one piece." Her hands slipped wetly over his ribs and to his belly. She worked lower and found what she sought just under the level of the water. "Is it because it's cold?"

"It's because I hurt like a son of a bitch," Slocum said. "And the cold."

Abigail laughed at this and sat back on the bank. He turned and looked at her with her knees pulled up and her skirt off the ground, giving him a view of her bloomers. She was lovely and enticing but he felt no stirrings at all. Perhaps in a few days, but right now, simple movement made him flinch.

"You are indeed in sad shape."

"Thanks," Slocum said dryly. He pulled himself out of the pool and shook like a dog. Abigail laughed and turned to keep from getting water in her eyes. Slocum took his time dressing, as much from the soreness that remained as to gauge Abigail's reaction.

By the time he settled his gun belt around his waist, he knew he wasn't going to ride off, intending never to see her again, as he had done before.

"The Paiutes won't come after us. There's little reason for them to," Slocum said, figuring this was true. Their war chief had been kicked in the head by Slocum's mare, but chiefs were voted in and out constantly. Another would take charge, and maybe even take the squaw that had caused so much trouble.

"William has a new idea on what he wants to do," she said.

"No more hunting?"

"Oh, he will hunt. He's out now, but he said something about wanting to see a real gold mine. That's nothing but a hole in the ground. I would much prefer to see the gold itself."

"Might be possible to do both," Slocum said. "There are mines to the north, up in the Sierra Nevadas."

"It sounds dreary. I would prefer to return to Virginia City. There were people having fun there."

Slocum said nothing to this. If either of them went back to the boomtown, they likely would have nooses dropped around their necks. There had already been too close a call in that regard for Slocum's comfort.

"I hear a horse. William must be back. Why don't you talk to him?"

"What are you going to do?"

Abigail grinned her wicked grin and said, "You look so refreshed, I think I might take a bath also. A long one. If you tire of listening to William, come back and join me." She impulsively pulled him to her and kissed him quickly. "Now go on, John. He will want to see you right away."

"And if he doesn't get his way, he gets mean," Slocum said.

Abigail's good humor drained away. She turned from him and began disrobing. As much as he wanted to watch, he knew he had to deal with Cheswick first. Slocum got back to the clearing as Cheswick hopped to the ground from horseback. He had bagged several small birds that might have been mountain quail. Before Slocum got a good look at them, Cheswick handed them to Quinton and snapped his fingers in Slocum's direction.

"You're back, my man. So good to see you again." Cheswick's tone almost made Slocum mount and ride out, but he doubted he could get back into the saddle without Quinton's help.

"At least this time, you've not out bagging Indian women," Slocum said, not trying to hide his contempt. "You could have gotten us all killed."

"Don't be ridiculous. I was only having sport with the savage. I didn't mean anything by it. Why, Abigail would never hear of such a thing as you're suggesting."

Slocum wondered what the hell that meant. Cheswick didn't seem the sort to think of anyone else, much less his sister.

"I killed their war chief. I doubt they'll be on our trail."

"That's the spirit, Slocum. Now," Cheswick said, wiping his hands on a small towel he carried, "I have decided to put some life into this expedition. I want to see a gold mine and share stories with the troglodytes who work in them."

"You want to get drunk with miners?"

"That's a rather crude way of putting it, but yes, you are right. I must adapt to these primitive conditions and learn how you . . . Colonials speak. Much cruder than in the polite society I am used to, I am sure, but it will be necessary for me to sample this wonderful country to the fullest."

"This is mining country," Slocum said slowly, "so there shouldn't be any trouble finding a mine to poke around in."

"Not just any mine," Cheswick said haughtily. "It must produce gold. I want to see it coming from the ground."

"I'll leave in the morning." Slocum hesitated, then asked, "Is that where you were heading? Into the mountains to find a mine?"

Cheswick smirked and nodded, then made shooing motions to dismiss Slocum. Again, the urge to simply ride out and keep going was great, but Slocum held back. He needed the money, no matter how annoying Cheswick was.

A few yards off, he ran into Quinton.

"Why'd he get the bee in his bonnet about seeing a working gold mine?"

Quinton looked uneasy, then peered past Slocum to be sure that his master did not overhear.

"A letter. He read a letter and jumped up, quite early this morning, yelling and storming about as if he were quite mad."

"Mad as a hatter or mad like a stepped-on dog?"

"I don't understand," Quinton said, although it was obvious he did.

"Where'd the letter come from? There's no delivery out here."

"He'd had it for some time but had never opened it. Perhaps the rush of events caused him to forget."

"Where'd he get the letter? Virginia City?"

"I believe that is correct," Quinton said.

Slocum left the servant and went to assemble the food he would need for the trail. He was hungrier than a bear coming out of hibernation, and he wasn't going to skimp on eating if Cheswick supplied the goods. Nothing but oatmeal and beans washed down with boiled coffee got tiresome after a week or two.

He rummaged through the camp supplies and took what he needed. Slocum intended to find a shady spot and sleep the rest of the day, but saw Abigail walking briskly from the direction of the stream. Her midnight black hair floated behind her like a garrison banner. Her stride long and her eyes ahead, she was so intent on going to speak with her brother that she never saw him. Slocum considered sidling over and eavesdropping, then got a better idea.

He would ride out of camp and not get caught up anymore in the quicksand that both Cheswicks provided in such abundance. He mounted, pleased that his body wasn't as sore as it had been, and headed northward. As he passed Cheswick's tent, he caught snippets of the conversation.

". . . you can't know for sure," Abigail said.

"The letter, my dear, the letter! What else can it mean?"

Slocum trotted out of earshot before he heard the woman's response. It was as he had thought. Someone had sold William Cheswick a bogus map showing the location of a surefire, can't-miss, riches-beyond-dreams-of-avarice gold mine. The Britisher could afford whatever he had paid, but Slocum hoped there wouldn't be trouble if the map led them to an already developed claim.

He rode steadily through the day, varying his speed from a slow walk to a trot to give the mare a chance to rest.

Slocum would have dismounted for a spell, but feared he might have trouble getting back in the saddle. Riding caused muscles he did not even know he had to ache. The Paiutes had worked him over better than if he'd been in a fifty-round bare-knuckles fight.

The valley broadened even more, then funneled into a well-traveled road going into the high country. From evidence he found along the road, more than one heavily laden wagon rolled this way every few days. The weeds were well crushed and the dirt packed down harder than stone.

"He's hunting for a mine. Maybe he should have given me the map so I could locate it and let him know the bad news, eh?" He patted his mare's neck. The horse nickered. "You're right," Slocum went on, the sound of his own voice soothing to the horse and filling a void. The wind had died down, and even the insects had stopped buzzing about in the heat of the afternoon. The world had gone to sleep and if Slocum had any sense, he would stop for a siesta, too. But he wanted to finish his scouting, fetch Cheswick, and collect his money.

The road into the foothills narrowed, but a dozen smaller tracks led in either direction. He rode into a pass and looked around. Behind lay the grassy valley, but ahead the country turned rockier and more suitable for mining. Slocum had spent too much time underground working in mines to find it anything but backbreaking and filthy. Herding cattle or farming was a far better way of making a living.

He began counting the crude signs marking the side roads, and stopped when he reached twenty. On the hillsides, miners had burrowed into the hard rock and left the tongues of dark tailings to scar the land. Most of these mines had been abandoned for some time, but Slocum saw glittering pyrite in the tailings from several higher up the side of one particular mountain, making him believe they were still being actively mined.

Reaching them would be the work of a day or longer because of the steep, twisting roads carved out of the rock itself. That didn't matter to Slocum. If anything, when Cheswick saw how difficult it would be to get into real mining country, it might dissuade him. From everything Slocum knew of the British lord, his employer was not a man to pass on his luxuries. The fancy-ass tent, servants, the huge larder in the wagon, the magnificent horses—all said that William Cheswick was not one to go without the finer things in life.

Slocum wheeled his horse about to retrace his path. He could camp at the edge of the valley and then reach Cheswick by noon the following day. Getting back here would be easy enough, even if actually reaching a mine would be difficult.

Or it would have been easy if a bullet didn't punch a hole in Slocum's Stetson to send it sailing.

9

Slocum didn't have to put his spurs to the mare's flanks. The horse already flew along the road, but Slocum slowed the headlong gallop, and eventually brought the horse to a dead halt. He turned about and studied the landscape behind him. As he looked, he ran his hand along the brim of his hat and shoved his finger through the new hole. If it rained anytime soon, he would have quite a leak.

"Rifle," he said, piecing together the details he had ignored before. He judged distances and the angle of the bullet as it had ripped through the hat brim, and found a spot high in the rocks where the sniper had to be hiding. Slowly drawing his own rifle from the saddle sheath, he sighted along the barrel and lined up the V sight with the front sight bead. He used his knees to hold his horse as still as possible. After the run, the mare was lathered up and edgy, but Slocum held steady enough to take the shot when it came.

The crown of a hat poked up. He fired. The hat went sailing through the air, and an instant later a man scrambled after it. Slocum fired again and brought the man down. The most he had done was to wing his ambusher, but it slowed down any chance of the man scrambling back into hiding.

Slocum yelled, "Move and I'll plug you! I'm good enough a shot for that."

He fired again when the man disobeyed. His shot was more lucky than skillful.

"Three aces," Slocum muttered, but this time his luck was good. His slug ripped the man's boot heel off and sent him tumbling downhill.

Trotting back, keeping his rifle ready, Slocum came to a spot along the road where he had a good shot at the man.

"Who the hell are you, and why're you shooting at me?"

"You're a damn claim jumper. You want to steal Ole Betsy from me."

"Who's that? Your woman?"

"My mine! You ain't playin' dumb. You come up here to take my mine from me. I ain't lettin' you. Not you or any of your belly-crawlin', terbacky-swallowin' sons o' bitches!"

"I don't want your mine," Slocum said. The old coot had been out in the sun too long. More likely, he had been alone so long that any other human he saw became an enemy out to steal his mine.

"Ever'body wants Ole Betsy. She's the best producin' mine in the whole of Nevada."

Slocum doubted that. The old man worked the claim by himself. Otherwise, his partner would have told him to behave himself. More likely, if the miner ever had a partner, he had come to a violent end and that demise had driven the survivor crazy.

"I'm looking for a big mine, one with lots and lots of miners working the claim," said Slocum.

"Did that snake Bold Max Carson send you? I tole him he cain't buy the Ole Betsy. I named 'er after my sweet ole ma, and she's been a real peach for me."

"Where's Bold Max Carson to be found?"

"Up at the Climax. Whole lot of them company boys workin' there." The old miner spat and looked defiant. "You go on up there and you see Charlie, you tell him I think he's a traitor fer leavin' me and the Ole Betsy and that he made a big mistake. The Betsy's gonna pour out the gold any day now. You tell him that!"

"He your partner?"

"My ex-partner. The Climax opens and he waltzes off to be paid a dollar a day and vittles and leaves me all by my lonesome. Well, the joke's on him. I'm gonna be rich!"

"Where's the Climax?"

The miner pointed farther along the road. "Nigh on ten miles that way. Take the mountain road up into the hills. Steep road, dangerous. Men fall off into the canyons all the time. But not Charlie. He's too cussed fer that!"

"And not Bold Max either?" Slocum almost laughed. Provoking the miner was too easy.

"He lured Charlie away with money. Gold dust, he says, but he pays his men with worthless greenbacks. Scrip! He pays his miners in paper when he's pullin' real gold from the rocks. But not as much as in Ole Betsy." The miner squinted suspiciously at Slocum. "You're not here to steal my mine?"

"All yours, old-timer," Slocum said. "A word of advice. Don't shoot at men traveling this road. One of them's likely to do more than shoot off the heel of your boot." Slocum sheathed his Winchester and waited for the miner to stalk off, grumbling as he went.

Slocum got back on the road with solid information about a large, profitable mining operation sure to satisfy Cheswick's need to see gold pulled from hard rock. Barely had he ridden a mile when he saw a rider far ahead of him. Something about the way the man sat his horse turned Slocum wary. He reached around and pulled his field glasses from his saddlebags. When he put them to his eyes, he saw a man staring back at him through another pair of field glasses.

"So you've turned up again like a bad penny," Slocum said softly. He was fairly sure he recognized the man ahead as the rider he had played cat and mouse with in the valley. He put away his binoculars and rode forward, not hurrying but not slowing either. He wanted to see what the mysterious rider would do.

It came as no surprise when the man finally lowered his own field glasses and galloped away, heading into the hills to the right of the road. When Slocum reached the spot where the man had ridden away, he dismounted, groaned at the effort, and stretched to work out the kinks in his muscles. He decided not to kneel and study the trail because standing again would be hard, with his ribs as bruised as they were. Slocum pulled his hat brim down to shield his eyes, and tried to find the rider in the midst of rocks and vegetation that stretched all the way to the top of a low ridge.

It took a considerable amount of willpower not to keep on his trail. Following anyone through such rocky terrain was difficult, but Slocum wondered why the man was so skittish. He wasn't up to any good, but unlike the crazy old miner, he hadn't shot at Slocum. This made Slocum decide to return to Cheswick and get the Britisher up to the Climax Mine so he could get a taste of another curious aspect of American culture. Let the rider spy all he wanted, as long as he didn't take potshots at Slocum.

After spending the night near a stream and sleeping fitfully because of his bruised body, Slocum rode back to Cheswick's camp. Although the ride was uneventful, he kept looking over his shoulder, and several times doubled back to see if he was being followed. If he was, whoever tracked him hid better than any Apache could. Slocum was satisfied he had returned to Cheswick without bringing a parade of others with him.

"You made good time, Slocum," Cheswick greeted. The

man wore a hunting jacket with a padded shoulder where
the butt of his elephant rifle could rest. Slocum didn't miss
how the rifle had crushed the leather patch from repeated
firing. "Did you find a big mine?"

"The Climax is supposed to have a dozen or so men
working it. That's a huge mine for this part of Nevada,"
Slocum said. He swung down to the ground, steadier now
than he had been even a day earlier. He would be back to
fighting trim before he knew it.

"The Climax," Cheswick said, rolling the name over and
over on his tongue as if he savored a fine wine. "That's it.
Yes, that's the one I must visit."

"With your wagons and gear, it'll be two or three days
of hard travel. Easy enough the first day getting out of the
valley. Then the road gets steep and narrow up into the
mountains."

"We can travel much lighter," Cheswick said, as if he
had already decided the matter before Slocum spoke.
"Quinton can stay here in this camp. You and I and Abigail
will ride on, with a pack animal or two."

"I'm not your servant," Slocum said after a moment of
thinking about what the man meant.

"You are my scout. I'm not sure I would trust you to
cook my meals. Abigail can do that."

Slocum started to ask if Abigail could cook in a kitchen,
much less on a campfire under the stars, but he held his
tongue. He wasn't averse to doing the cooking, but he drew
the line at all the other menial chores Quinton took care of
in the camp.

"You see anything of the two that hightailed it during
the Paiute attack?" Slocum asked.

"What other two? Oh, the scurrilous servants who abandoned me when danger reared its ugly head? No, I've seen
nothing of them and if I do, they're in for a sound thrash-
ing." Cheswick clenched his hands as if he had one of the
servant's necks under his fingers. He relaxed when he real-

ized Slocum was staring at him and his mock execution. "Go on. Pack up. We'll hit the trail, as you say, right away."

"Tomorrow at daybreak," Slocum said. "I'm tuckered out, and my horse needs to rest."

"Get another. I don't know why you ride that nag." Cheswick looked as if he might be sick as he eyed the mare standing patiently a few yards away.

"She suits me," Slocum said. "Dawn."

"Yes, yes, dawn tomorrow," Cheswick said. As Slocum went to find himself a spot to make his own camp, he saw Cheswick take a sheet of paper from a pocket and stare at it. A slow smile curled his lips. Then he put the paper back where it had been. He walked away, whistling some jaunty tune Slocum almost recognized.

"The trail is quite steep, isn't it, John?" Abigail Cheswick looked up the sheer face of the mountain at the road painstakingly clawed onto its face.

"The Climax Mine's almost at the summit," he said. "We're rested enough to make the entire trip on the road by noon."

"That's three hours," she said uneasily. Abigail turned to her brother and clutched at his arm. "Do we have to go, William? All of us?"

"Yes, my dear, *all* of us. You heard what Slocum said about the murderous miner taking shots at him."

"But he was miles back down the road, and we didn't see him." She looked up apprehensively at the steep road.

"There, there, my dear," Cheswick said, pulling her close and giving her a long kiss on the lips that Slocum found disconcerting, though Abigail did not resist. They broke off the kiss. Cheswick looked at Slocum with a bravado that would have meant a gunfight if any Westerner had flashed that look his way. That look dared Slocum to say a word, to make a move.

"Let's ride," Slocum said. This produced a sharp laugh on Cheswick's part. He and Abigail exchanged looks that Slocum couldn't decipher and didn't much want to. For all her beauty, Abigail Cheswick had strange ways about her.

Cheswick rode ahead, letting Slocum hang back with Abigail between them on the narrow trail. Slocum guessed a narrow wagon might go up and down the road to supply the mine and miners at the top, but anything larger would tumble down the mountainside.

"I'm so fearful of heights," Abigail said. "When William and I went to Switzerland, I could not bear to go up the slopes and stayed in Zurich." She looked pale and kept her eyes averted from the increasingly large drop on their right.

"You don't have any business up there," Slocum said, pointing to the area where the Climax Mine chewed away at the mountain. Clouds drifted low and occasionally obscured the area. "Wait at the base of the mountain. The old coot who took a shot at me won't bother you."

"I'll keep going," she said. Abigail swallowed hard, then resolve flooded into her. Slocum saw her shoulders pull back and her jaw tense. "It's something I want to do."

They rode in silence for an hour, each lost in his or her own thoughts, with Slocum thinking a great deal about how vulnerable any rider was on the way to the summit. The road curled halfway around the mountain, giving a drop of a hundred feet or more into a canyon. From what Slocum could see below, several men and their horses had tumbled off the road here. Their picked-white bones gleamed below in the noonday sun, giving mute testimony to the dangers of mining—and just getting to the mine. He didn't bother pointing them out to Abigail, and Cheswick rode ahead as if he couldn't wait to get to the top. Slocum shared that ambition, but probably not for the same reason. He was tired and still ached. What Cheswick's reasons were, he kept to himself.

"Men ahead," Abigail said. "William, wait. Be careful!"

Her brother ignored her and rode directly toward the tight knot of men dressed in flannel shirts and canvas pants, as if this was a uniform and they were all dutiful soldiers. In a way, Slocum knew, this was close to the truth. Working in a mine was cold, dirty work and took a toll on clothing as well as men. The way they dressed was both durable and warm.

Slocum touched his six-shooter but did not draw. Miners were notoriously clannish, and the ones that didn't work in companies turned into hermits, like the one he had met at the base of the road.

"I say, old chaps, put down those weapons. I am here to experience your pitiful condition."

Slocum stopped beside Cheswick and leaned forward. Left to his own devices, Cheswick would have the miners in a fury and throwing them off the side of the mountain.

"Which of you's Charlie?" Slocum asked. "I got a message from his former partner down below at the Ole Betsy Mine."

"That's me. I'm Charlie Gustav." A man elbowed his way forward. "What's the message?"

"Your former partner apologizes." Slocum had no idea what had caused the break. It might have been the lack of gold in the mine, but more likely it was something personal. Men turned into sandpaper, grinding away at each other until tempers rubbed thin and arguments erupted on a daily schedule about the same things.

"The hell you say. You tell that old fool that he's plumb crazy and I ain't returnin'!"

"I'll convey the message when I can. Just happened I was coming this way. Otherwise, I wouldn't have ever run into him."

"He knowed you was comin' up here?"

Slocum nodded.

"I'll be danged. Maybe he's not as loony as I thought."

Charlie and two others put their heads together and argued. Slocum couldn't care less about the subject of the argument. All he knew was that by establishing some rapport he had defused a powder keg Cheswick had insisted on lighting.

To Cheswick, he said softly, "They're nervy types. You've got to go slow getting to know them."

"Liquor!" Cheswick called. "I want to drink with you—" He jerked when Slocum elbowed him in the ribs to keep him from insulting the miners again.

"You wanna split a bottle with us? How come?" Charlie peered up at Cheswick. "We ain't got nuthin' you want."

"Your company," Cheswick said. "I desire your company."

"The Climax Mine's not fer sale," Charlie said. "Even if it was, we can't sell it. We only work for Mr. Dumont, and he's over in San Francisco."

"He thinks you meant the company that owns the mine," Slocum explained when he saw Cheswick's confusion.

"You, my good man, I want to drink with you. And you and you!" Cheswick pulled out two bottles of rye from his saddlebags and held them up, one in each hand.

A cheer went up. There had never been a miner who wouldn't partake of a free drink, no matter the source. Slocum had to admit Cheswick had won them over after a rocky start. The Brit dropped off his horse and called over his shoulder, "Be a good fellow, Slocum, and tend my horse."

"John, please," Abigail said from behind him. She saw how Slocum had tensed. He had told Cheswick he wasn't another servant and wouldn't be treated like one. "It's his way. He doesn't know any better."

"He should learn," Slocum said, but he bent down and grabbed the reins. He led the horse to a trough and let it drink. He swung from the saddle and stretched.

"I could work out some of those kinks. Or perhaps I could straighten out parts that needed it," Abigail said.

"That the payment for tending his horse?" Slocum spoke more harshly than he had intended, and Abigail recoiled. To his surprise, she smiled and nodded.

"When we get a chance. It seems I am something of a celebrity like William."

Slocum looked past Abigail, and saw a half dozen miners staring at her. Women in mining camps were as rare as hen's teeth.

"Come on," Slocum said after letting his horse drink. He led the mare and Cheswick's stallion to a hitching post, then helped Abigail down. "We should see what trouble your brother's got himself into."

They went to a building about ready to fall down. There wasn't a square joint anywhere—not in the doorway or the roof. The prevailing wind had worked its airy magic too long and was gradually pushing the clapboard building flat. The men inside the rude mess hall weren't the least bit interested in that. The bottles making the rounds were the only things in their lives.

"These are notable drinking companions, Slocum. Come, join us." William grinned crookedly and said to his sister, "You may join us also, Abigail."

"I'll watch," she said. Her nose wrinkled in distaste, as much at the miners as at her brother's attitude toward her.

Slocum settled down next to Charlie, and listened to the men gossiping like women at a quilting bee. He realized that Cheswick was doing the same thing, prodding with a question or two now and then, but mostly letting the men spill all the details of their dreary lives.

"How come you're not in the mine working?" Slocum asked.

"Well, it's like this," Charlie said. "We been workin' so danged hard, we need more dynamite to blast and our tools have gone dull. We got explosives and files to sharpen our picks on the way up."

"Do tell," Slocum said. The men hadn't been loafing

when Cheswick had ridden up. They were outside the mine sorting ore that had been pulled from the side of the mountain. Some chore always existed, even if it didn't involve being buried under tons of rock.

"Best danged freighter in the territory's bringin' ever'thin' we need up the road."

"We didn't see anybody. How long's it going to be until he gets supplies to you?"

"You came up from the valley side. The road goes down the mountain the other way, into Virginia City."

Slocum tried not to react. He had not realized the Climax Mine was so near the source of much of his trouble.

"How long's it take to get up from town?"

"A day, maybe two, but ole Pete's a masterful driver. He can git them mules of his to pull twice what anyone else can. And fast!"

"Sounds like the kind of freighter you want supplying you," Slocum said, his attention drifting to the others at the long, stained table that was as poorly built as the building itself. Whatever carpenter had put together the furniture and building had lacked real skill, or maybe was a tad nearsighted.

"Yup. Be here by noon tomorrow, or so he says. That lets us have a holiday. Yer buddy down there, he's a pistol, ain't he?"

Slocum saw that Cheswick was singing a bawdy song and had his arms around the shoulders of the men on either side of him. Standing behind him, Abigail had her arms crossed and was glaring at him.

"Slocum!" Cheswick bellowed from the other end of the table. "Tomorrow morn's the time. They'll let me go into the mine and perhaps even bring out a nugget."

"Big as a hen's egg," said the miner on Cheswick's right. This produced a round of laughter. "Cain't let him take anything bigger 'n that or it comes out of our pay!"

This caused even more boisterous laughter. Somewhere

in the crowd of miners, a supervisor would watch to be sure such a thing never happened, but it was perfect for joshing the generous foreigner.

Slocum actually sampled the whiskey when the almost empty bottle made its way around the table to him. After Cheswick saw this mine, there'd be no more reason for him to employ a scout.

Slocum jumped to his feet, hand going to the six-shooter at his hip when the door slammed open and a bull-throated roar filled the room.

"What the hell's goin' on here? Why ain't you all workin' instead of sittin on your fat asses?"

The man was short and built like a brick shit house and looked as mad as anyone Slocum had ever seen.

"That there's our foreman, Bold Max," muttered Charlie from the table. "We're in fer it now."

10

"I'm gonna dock the lot of you a day's pay for bein' drunk on the job!"

"Mr. Carson," Slocum said, getting up. "It's not their fault. My employer, William Cheswick, is a traveler from England and heard about the Climax Mine."

"So?" Bold Max Carson thrust out his chin like a bulldog and glared up at Slocum.

"He wanted to see the famed operation and meet its supervisor. That'd be you."

"Why?"

"You're the most famous mine foreman in Nevada, that's why," Slocum said. "He's thinking of expanding the mines he owns and might need you to supervise a half dozen operations this size."

"Me?"

Slocum decided Bold Max had earned his nickname doing something other than speaking. He motioned for Abigail to come over.

"Lord William and his sister, Lady Abigail, are touring the West hunting for properties to buy. They're from England."

Bold Max eyed Cheswick and dismissed him as a fop, but the mine foreman couldn't as easily take his eyes off Abigail. The woman moved like a dream and acted like a princess as she worked to charm him. Bold Max had probably never seen her ilk before, and she reveled in behaving like royalty.

As Carson and Abigail talked, or rather as Abigail talked and the foreman listened, Cheswick took Slocum by the arm and moved him to the side of the room.

"Well done, Slocum. You've quite a quick wit about you."

"Any smoothing of ruffled feathers is going to be done by your sister," Slocum said.

"Oh, she is quite good at that," Cheswick said. "I have discovered that a freight wagon is on the way here from Virginia City."

"Name's Pete and the miners think highly of him. So?"

"Ride down the trail and meet him. I believe he is carrying something of great value to me."

"What'd that be?" Slocum looked suspiciously at the Brit.

"That's not for you to question," Cheswick said sharply. "Do as I request. There'll be a bonus in it for you if this Pete arrives with the special package."

"Does this have something to do with the letter you got?" Slocum enjoyed seeing the blood drain from Cheswick's face. He opened his mouth, but no words came out. He clamped his mouth shut, and then took a deep breath to collect his thoughts.

"My affairs are mine and mine alone. Do not intrude where you have no business poking your nose."

"All you want is for me to guard Pete and his shipment?"

"That's all."

Slocum nodded. This would be the final time he was pushed around. From what Charlie and the other miners said about Pete, he was a decent fellow and the best freighter in Nevada. Slocum preferred his company, sight unseen, to Cheswick's.

"Go on. Ride down the trail so you can accompany him when it's daylight."

"If the road down to Virginia City is as narrow and tricky as the one we took getting here, riding at night might be dangerous."

"You're being paid well. Do it, or are you frightened of such a nocturnal sojourn?"

"You talk about big pay, but I haven't seen a thin dime of it so far."

"Here. Take this as an advance against your future work." Cheswick pulled out a wad of greenbacks big enough to choke a cow and peeled off fifty dollars. He held it out for Slocum to take. Slocum saw a conflict of wills building, and made no move to take it because he was sure Cheswick would snatch it back at the last instant and add another condition to it, just to show who was the boss.

"Well, don't you want it?" By asking, Cheswick had lost a little status, but he could still pull the money away if Slocum grabbed for it.

"You can hand it to me anytime you want, and I'll be on my way."

Reluctantly, Cheswick lost the silent battle of wills and held it out for Slocum. If he had jerked it away now, he would have looked like a fool. Slocum tucked the scrip into the vest pocket with the elephant rifle cartridge. Without another word, he left.

Let Cheswick have his tour of a closed-in, dusty, dangerous mine. Slocum preferred the open sky above him. He found the mine's stables, tended his horse, and made sure the mare ate well from the sparse bin of oats before mounting and heading onto the road that spiraled down the mountain's other side. As he rode, Slocum felt increasingly uneasy. He ought to be riding away from Virginia City, not toward it. Mac wasn't the sort to forget a slight. His brother's death would still be high on his list of wrongs to avenge.

After an hour of riding on the uneven, narrow road, Slocum wondered how anyone could drive a wagon of any size along it, yet he saw wagon wheel indentations that showed someone did. Pete had to be one hell of a fine driver. But orders from Cheswick or not, Slocum wasn't able to ride much farther. His mare began to stumble, which worried him. He couldn't see the precipice by the roadside, but knew there were probably as many picked-clean skeletons of unwary travelers here as there had been on the other side of the mountain.

When he came to a widened spot in the road designed to allow two wagons to pass, he decided it was time to stop for the night. This wasn't the most comfortable place he had ever slept in, but it was far from the worst. He prepared a camp, ate from the victuals from Cheswick's supplies, and then stretched out. Overheard, the stars shone down on him, but he didn't feel at ease with them the way he usually did. Slocum sat up and looked around. He thought he heard a horse neighing in the distance, but might have been wrong. The mountains changed sounds and made identification tricky at times.

The memory of the mystery rider returned, but Slocum doubted the man had followed along the road. There might be other riders, coming from Virginia City in a posse. Slocum forced himself to stop dwelling on that possibility. As mad as Mac might be, he still had to round up a posse. Miners were miners because they liked being underground. Spending any time on the trail would make them as jumpy as being underground made Slocum.

He lay back and pulled his blanket around his shoulders. Sleep came hard and when he awoke just before dawn, he was barely rested. Still, he was on the trail again and had some folding money in his pocket. Things could be worse.

He ate a cold breakfast of jerky and some hardtack before resuming his trip. As he rode, he thought he heard a horse again. Look as he might, he couldn't find the source of the noise.

He had ridden barely an hour when he heard a whip snapping and mules braying. He dismounted, went to the verge of the road, and peered down at the switchback fifty feet under him. A wagon filled the roadbed from side to side and scraped the mountainside as it worked its way upward along the road. The driver had a big-brimmed floppy hat pulled down low on his face, and his words were mumbled as he cussed at his team.

Slocum sat and waited for the freighter to reach him rather than continuing downward. He was at another widened spot in the road, though there wasn't much extra space as the wagon crept toward him.

"What are you doing blocking the road, you bloody sot?"

Slocum's eyes narrowed as he studied the driver.

"You named Pete? I was told to come down from the mine and escort you back."

"Why? Nobody's ever given me a guard before."

Pete had his hat pulled down around his ears, but his words were muffled and a little slurred because of a bandage wrapped across his right eye and taped to his left jaw, hiding a goodly portion of his face.

"You're a Brit," Slocum said.

"Bully for you, you blithering dolt. Of course I am, and you're an ignorant Yank."

"That wasn't the side I fought on."

"Then you're a bloody Johnny Reb," Pete corrected. "To me, it doesn't matter. That wasn't our war."

"I'm just another Colonial," Slocum said. To his surprise, Pete sat a little straighter, then laughed heartily.

"You got a sense of humor, fella. They sent you down, you say?"

"You've got cargo I'm supposed to protect."

"You can ride along if you like. Just don't go smoking."

"Explosives," Slocum said. He looked into the wagon bed to get an idea what Pete might be carrying that was so important to Cheswick. The large pile covered with canvas had to be cases of dynamite. The rest were crates of food and other necessities for the miners. "This all of it?"

"The lot, unless some bounced out on one of the turns. I take 'em fast, you know."

Slocum laughed again. Every inch of this road had to be fought for and earned by the freighter's skill and the strength of his four mules.

"Tie your horse to the back and climb up," said Pete. "The mules won't notice your extra weight. If they do, you can get out and push and they'll thank you kindly."

"Never saw a mule that'd do that," Slocum said. He gingerly climbed into the wagon and sat on the hard bench beside Pete. The freighter canted his head to the side and peered at him with a bloodshot left eye.

"You banged up?" Pete asked.

"Not as much as you. What happened?"

"Pub fight. The other bloke had a knife. I didn't see it until it was too late. Now the doc says I won't be seeing anything out of that eye this side of the Pearly Gates."

"How'd you end up in Nevada? This is a mighty long way from England."

"Nothing for me there but heartache. My wife-to-be died and I didn't have anything to hold me there, so I decided to see the world."

"Now you've got to see it one-eyed," Slocum said.

"I see more with one eye than most of the miners around here do with two. Never saw a bunch so narrow-minded, 'less it was my family. They were a—whoa!"

Pete stood, put one foot against the edge of the wagon, and used his full weight and strength to stop the mules. As they stopped pulling, he kicked out and braced his foot against the brake to keep from rolling backward.

Slocum tried to figure out what was wrong, but saw nothing. The wagon had rolled along with only creaks and groans, which was usual for this rough a road.

"What's wrong?" Pete asked.

"Can't say. I get this feeling there's someone else around but nobody passed me on the way up," Slocum said. "That means it has to be someone on the way down." He couldn't shake the notion of the mystery rider from over in the valley. Whoever that person was, he had taken an interest in Slocum that was bordering on the unhealthy—for one of them.

Pete sank back down onto the wood bench, snapped the reins, and got the mules pulling before he released the brake. The wagon lurched, and they continued their upward climb.

"I've been at this for almost six months, and it never feels natural to me. There's always something worrying me."

"That's all? Six months? You drive like you were born with reins in your hand," Slocum said.

"There wasn't much else I was good at. I knew animals. Rode back in England, but there wasn't much call for a steeplechase rider out here. The mules took a fancy to me, and I found myself the only route no one else would drive."

"Is the pay good?"

"Better than the money I get from back home," Pete said.

"Somebody sends you money?"

"I'm what they call a remittance man. You know the term?"

"You're the second one I've come across in the past week," Slocum said.

"The West is crawling with our kind," Pete said. He applied the brake, gingerly guided the mules around a sharp bend, and started to snap the reins to keep the team pulling hard when a loud crack sounded. At first Slocum thought one of the yokes had broken. Then he saw the lead mule stagger to the side.

"Watch it!" Slocum cried.

It was too late. The mule's left legs both slid over the verge. As the heavy animal fell, still in harness, it took the other lead mule with it. Then the wagon began to roll and slide sideways at the same time.

"We're going over the edge!"

Those were the last words Slocum heard from Pete before the wagon skidded off the road and sent them both tumbling into space.

11

Slocum remembered falling and then an impact that rattled him hard. The next thing he felt was sharp pain throughout his body. He thought the Paiutes had caught him again and whaled away on him. One eyelid flickered and finally opened so he could stare up at the bright blue Nevada sky. A puffy white cloud built and died before he could force open the second eye, and this took some work since it had been glued shut by dried blood.

Forcing his elbows down, he lifted his body enough to look around. The wagon had disintegrated as it bounced off the mountainside and had cast splinters around.

"The only good thing I can tell," came a weak voice, "is that the dynamite didn't blow. The boys at the Climax are going to get mighty hungry before there's another shipment of food, though."

"They can do without the dynamite," Slocum said, sitting up all the way and trying to get his feet under him. He lay on a steep incline and slipped and slid a ways downhill before he dug in his heels and got some purchase. "Food's another matter."

"Bold Max will have my head on a pike for this," Pete said. He had looked chewed up and spit out before the plunge. Now his head bandage was soaked in fresh blood, and his clothing had been shredded by a fall through a pine tree's limbs. Slocum studied the matter, and realized this might have saved the freighter's life. If he had missed the tree, he would have fallen another forty feet through jagged-edged rocks.

Twisting around and wincing at the pain, Slocum looked above him on the slope. He had been damned lucky, too. He had followed the wagon down rather than being under it, and had skidded on a rough patch of rock that had slowed him enough to prevent a further tumble down the hillside.

"Anything to salvage?" Slocum called over to Pete.

"Nothing I see. Bloody mules are all dead, I hope. I'd hate to think they were somewhere I couldn't see and injured."

Slocum listened hard, but heard nothing but the wind blowing through the pine that had saved Pete's life. The mules had probably died at the spot where each had hit the mountainside, and then their lifeless bodies had slid on below.

"They might be on the lower switchback on the road."

"That'd be a gory bit of it, a traveler coming along and finding four dead mules blocking the road," Pete said. "You need help? You're a bloody fright."

Slocum moved carefully, testing for broken ribs. Amazingly, he felt no worse now than he had after escaping the Indians. He hurt like a rotten tooth, but all his bones were intact. His clothing was torn, and he bled from a dozen shallow scratches. Otherwise, he was no worse for the fall.

"Think my horse is still up on the road," Slocum said, peering up. "I saw something peek over the edge of the road and duck back."

"One good twitch of the head's all it would take to get

free of the wagon. I hope your horse is all right. She looked to be a feisty mare."

"Sturdy, with heart," Slocum said. He began working along the slope to reach Pete. The freighter had claimed he was all right, but Slocum saw a deep cut that bled freely.

"You go on up," Pete said. "Throw me a rope and pull me up. I'm not sure I can climb with my leg like this." He rubbed his right leg where the gash ran from thigh to knee.

"I'll see about stopping the bleeding. You might be too weak to loop the rope around you if you keep bleeding like that."

Pete groaned as Slocum ripped broad strips of his canvas pants leg away from the wound and used the fabric to fasten a tourniquet just above where the flesh parted.

"I've seen some bad wounds in my day. You'll live."

"Not if you talk my ear off. Can you make it to the road by yourself?"

"Don't start a game of solitaire. You won't finish before I drop you the rope."

Slocum made sure the tourniquet was set, slapped Pete on the shoulder, and then began climbing. His muscles protested every inch upward, but he drove his toes into the loose rock and found more solid footing. He had climbed mountains before, and knew to always keep three secure points while he moved the fourth. Bit by bit, he worked his way toward the edge of the road. From this vantage point, he saw how the road had been blasted out of solid mountain. So much work was a silent testament to how profitable the Climax Mine was.

When he was only a few feet below the road, his mare poked her head over and looked down at him. Her big brown eyes accused him of annoying her. He had to agree. He wished there hadn't been any trouble with the mule.

He got both hands on the solid edge of the road and heaved, pulling himself up so he could turn and flop flat. The horse came over and nuzzled him. Slocum got to his feet and patted the horse's neck by way of thanks for the greeting.

As he reached for the rope slung at his saddle, he paused. Staying alive and then struggling up the mountain-side had occupied his thoughts until this moment. Curious, he walked up the road to the spot where the mule had tumbled over. A large splotch of blood confirmed his memory of what had happened.

Someone had shot the lead mule, and it had stumbled and gone over the edge, taking the wagon, Pete, and Slocum with it. He looked around, but saw no one. The stretch of road from around the bend was straighter than most. A sniper might have taken a clean shot from that range, but Slocum couldn't figure out who would want the dynamite shipment to the mine stopped. Other than the food, Pete had said nothing else was aboard.

He went back to his horse, fastened one end of the rope around the saddle horn, and swung the loop on the other end around as if he intended to rope a steer. He peered down at Pete.

"You ready?"

"Ready as I'll ever be. My leg's turning colder than a witch's tit. I'm going to need you to tend it when I get back to the top."

"Here it comes." Slocum dropped the rope, and Pete fumbled to get it around his body. A quick tug told Slocum the freighter was ready to make the trip back up the slope a lot slower than he had gone down.

The mare began backing away, and Slocum kept the rope from abrading on the roadway's sharp rock edge. Foot by foot, Pete got closer, until Slocum grabbed, caught an outstretched arm, and pulled the man up to safety. For a moment, Pete lay on the road, then rolled over and pointed.

"I'll loosen it a mite," Slocum said as he worked at the knot on the tourniquet. If it stayed on too long, Pete would lose the leg. He would be a real sight then, one eye and one leg. Carefully releasing the pressure, Slocum was pleased to find that the wound had clotted. No new blood bubbled up.

"Think I'll be all right?"

"Right as rain, except for the tongue-lashing Bold Max is likely to give you for losing his shipment," Slocum joshed. He got his arm around Pete and helped the man to stand. "You be all right for a moment while I get my horse?"

"Been a while since I've ridden, but it'll be a real treat. My arse is flat from being bounced on that wagon bench seat."

Slocum coiled his rope and went to fasten it back on the saddle. He caught up the reins, and had turned to lead the horse back to where Pete stood on one leg when another shot rang out. Pete looked at Slocum, his face blank. The bullet had gone from one side of the man's head to the other. Pete took a single step and once more plunged over the edge of the cliff. This time, Slocum knew the freighter wasn't going to be alive when he finally stopped tumbling down the steep slope.

His hand went to his six-shooter and he drew. The shooter had to be nearby since the road worked its way around the bend not twenty feet away. A stone tumbled down on Slocum's hat brim and bounced away. Going into a crouch, he shoved his hat back off his head so it dangled by its string around his neck. He aimed uphill at where the road curled back around the mountain at a higher level.

All he saw was a blur of movement as a rifle barrel was pulled out of sight. He vaulted onto his mare and got the horse trotting along the narrow road. With the stone face close to his right arm to make the shot from above more difficult, Slocum rounded the bend and started down the long stretch of road toward the next turn.

"Son of a bitch," he cried. At the far turn, he saw the rider he had spotted back in the valley. Until now, the rider had only watched. Now he had killed an unarmed man. Slocum opened fire and drove the rider out of sight around the turn in the road.

Wanting to gallop, but fearing that a single stumble might doom him and his horse, Slocum rode as fast as he dared, reached the turn in the road, and started up another steep stretch. By the time he got to the spot where he had seen the rifle barrel, his horse was flagging. Slocum hated to let Pete's killer get away, but had no choice but to slow and walk the mare. Before the top of the steep uphill stretch, Slocum dismounted and walked alongside his horse.

He rounded another bend and cautiously looked for the mysterious rider. Nothing. He mounted and had to proceed slowly. The altitude and the hard riding over the past couple days had drained the stamina from his horse. He eventually got to the level area around the Climax Mine and hunted for someone to call to.

The road down the back of the mountain was the only place a rider could have gone since there were no side roads to the summit. Slocum swung about and started down the road. The sniper had to have come this way.

Or had he?

Slocum drew rein and looked around the mine site. He was sure he had properly identified the rider as the same one he had encountered in the valley at the base of the mountain. That meant the man wasn't a miner. If he was, he'd have been away from his work too long and would have been noticed. But he might be hiding.

Working his way past the leaning mess hall and toward sturdier sheds designed to hold dynamite, Slocum hunted for any trace of the rider. When he didn't see anything, he turned and went back to the road leading to the valley where he had first spotted the rider.

He trotted past the mouth of the mine as men were coming out from a day's work. Charlie waved at him and several others called his name, but Slocum had no time to waste. He kept his head down and rode as fast as his horse could take him. If he found a cutback on the road where he could look at a lower stretch, he might do to the sniper what had been done to Pete. Slocum wasn't above putting a slug or two into a murderous owlhoot's back.

He left the miners behind and rounded the first bend in the road. It was getting dark and he feared a misstep on his horse's part would doom them both. He finally realized that twilight was rapidly draining the daylight, leaving only darkness behind. Forced to dismount and walk, he kept moving for more than an hour. The whole while, he seethed at such cold-blooded killing. Pete had been unarmed and unable to defend himself.

Slocum knew he dared not turn the murderer over to the law when he caught him. He was still wanted for Renfro's killing back in Virginia City. Mac—or the marshal—wouldn't much care what he had done lawfully if they could pin Renfro's murder on him.

Finally forced to stop, Slocum sat on a rock and fumed while his horse rested. He might not be able to continue until morning. But once he got on the trail, he would not stop until Pete's killer was a dead man. Taking the law into his own hands wasn't something he thought much of, but he saw no other way of meting out justice.

He ate a cold dinner, wished he had watered his horse before leaving the Climax site, and finally leaned back against the rocky face of the cliff to his left and closed his eyes. Scenes of vengeance filled his dreams in which he satisfactorily ended the mystery rider's life in a hail of gunfire and a welter of shouted curses.

Slocum was slow to come awake to the realization that the gunshots were not real but the curses were.

He got to his feet and saw three riders coming down the road from up on the mountain, holding sputtering torches high over their heads to light the trail.

He recognized Bold Max and Charlie. The third man was dressed as a miner.

"Here he is, boss. I see him," Charlie cried out.

"You spotted him?" Slocum went to the edge of the road and looked over into utter darkness. He needed one of their torches if they had located Pete's killer.

"Where?" Slocum shouted. "I don't see him anywhere."

By then, the trio was upon him. When he saw their leveled six-shooters, he realized that he was their quarry. He slowly raised his hands so they wouldn't fill him full of lead.

12

"We thought you was a friendly sorta fella," Charlie said, his gun hand shaking. Slocum watched in the flickering torchlight as the miner fought with the temptation to squeeze the trigger. "Just goes to show how wrong you kin be, I reckon."

"Shut up," Bold Max said. He motioned with his six-gun for Slocum to mount. They had stripped him already of his Colt Navy and knife from the top of his boot.

"What's going on?" Slocum demanded. "I'm after the man who shot Pete. He shot a mule, we got back to the road, and then he shot Pete in the head."

"We heard the shots, and we went back and found the body. It had to be you. There wasn't nobody else on the road," Charlie said. "You was tryin' to escape, that's what you was doin'."

"I was after Pete's killer," Slocum said, trying to keep the anger from his tone. "He rode toward the mine and down this side of the mountain. If I'd killed Pete, why would I come this way? I'd have gone straight down the road to Virginia City and out of the territory."

"Reckon we'll find out why you wanted to come past us."

"To thumb his nose at us," suggested the third man.

Slocum had seen death in men's eyes before. This miner stared at him as if he were ready to kill on the spot. It probably had nothing to do with thinking he had killed Pete. The miner wanted to see someone die, and Slocum was on the wrong end of the gun.

"Back to camp," said Bold Max.

"There was someone on the trail ahead of me, going to the valley. He's the one who shot Pete."

"Ain't seen nobody but you go through the mine yard. Don't know what you had against Pete, but he was a good man. Snuck me whiskey now and then, too. For a Brit, he was a regular fella." Charlie's hand shook harder as he restrained himself from shooting Slocum.

The only one who remained in charge of his emotions was Bold Max Carson, and Slocum had the feeling that the animosity bubbling up from the mine foreman was enough to kill.

They rode back into the camp, which was lit with the sputtering pitch torches, giving an unreal look to everyone assembled. Slocum looked around for either Abigail or her brother, but they were nowhere to be seen. Rough hands dragged Slocum from the saddle, and he was buffeted about as grimy hands swung to hit him.

"Don't," Bold Max said gruffly. "He's our prisoner. We hold him for the marshal. Charlie, get on down to Virginia City and fetch that no-account."

"The marshal?"

"Hell, any of them lawmen'll do. The marshal, the sheriff, any of 'em. I want this varmint to stand trial right away. I don't want him in my camp one second longer 'n needed."

The miners punched at Slocum, but did him no real harm. He knew better than to argue with a mob. If he said something to anger them more, they were likely to string him up or just throw him over a cliff to his death. Little by little, he was shoved toward a shed. One miner opened the door, and two others grabbed Slocum by the arms and bodily threw him inside. He crashed into the rear of the shed, and found himself locked inside before he could recover.

Pressing his hands against the walls convinced him a different carpenter had built this building. If it had been constructed like the mess hall, he would have been free in a few seconds. He sat on an empty dynamite crate, and realized that Pete was bringing more explosives that would have been stored here. A quick check of the boxes failed to turn up any dynamite. Glum, Slocum sat on a crate and tried to think things through.

Even if he had found a stick or two, using it would have killed him. Being trapped inside a closed structure like this would have caused the blast to crush him to bloody jelly smeared on the walls. He tried scuffing the floor, but it was too hard to dig in even if he had a shovel. Windowless, the shed was as sturdy as a wooden structure got—and he had seen the heavy padlock on the door when they had shoved him inside. The lock kept out miners as surely as it now held him prisoner inside.

After trying the walls and floor, Slocum stood on a crate and pushed hard against the roof, hoping it might not have been fastened down as firmly as the rest of the shed panels. All he succeeded in doing was sending waves of pain throughout his body. He had been battered and beaten too much to be successful in escaping this way, even if the roof had only been laid onto the top of the walls.

He sank into a corner, legs drawn up as he considered what to do. If Bold Max had his way, a necktie party might be avoided. That still meant Slocum ended up in Virginia City where a murder accusation already awaited him. The Mountain of Gold barkeep wouldn't put much store in such a thing as a fair trial, not that a trial mattered much. Slocum couldn't prove he was innocent and any jury would be full of Mac's friends.

Taking a nail from an empty crate, he began scratching away at the door where the hinges were fixed in the sturdy frame. His progress was slow, but he was not going to give up. After an hour, he heard sounds outside and tensed. He held the blunt nail like a tiny knife. It wasn't much of a weapon, but if Charlie or the others had taken it into their heads to ignore their foreman and bring what they thought was justice to this part of Nevada, he would fight. A quick slash might give him the chance to grab a six-shooter.

The key grated noisily in the padlock. Slocum pictured the hasp falling open. The hinges screeched as the door opened. Slocum had tensed to explode outward when he saw Abigail Cheswick silhouetted in the doorway.

"Hurry, John. There's no time. We've got to get away."

"This is the second time you've got me out of a cell," he said.

"There's no time. The guard fell asleep. I had to act fast, but I don't know when he's going to wake up."

"Where's your brother?"

"Don't worry about him. He's already gone."

"He left you?" Slocum started to complain more, but Abigail pressed her finger against his lips to quiet him.

"I'll explain after we get away."

"The man who killed Pete rode back toward the valley. If we—"

"Not that way. To Virginia City. It's our only chance. Trust me, John, or they'll catch us."

She grabbed his hand and pulled him along to where his mare and her stallion were already saddled. Abigail mounted easily and waited for him.

"I need my six-shooter," he said.

"In your saddlebags. You can get it and your knife later, after we've put some miles between us and this mine."

Slocum gripped the pommel, got his foot in the stirrup, and heaved. He needed a few shots of whiskey to kill the pain more than he needed his six-gun right now. He settled down and followed Abigail from the mining camp. He looked at the road leading toward the valley, but Abigail had already hit the trail retracing Pete's route from Virginia City. Something bothered him about this area. He looked around, thinking Bold Max might have put a sentry on the road, but he saw nothing and heard less. At this altitude, even the usual wildlife fell silent. His study of the landscape turned upward to a spot higher on the slope. He made a few quick estimates, rode to the side of the road, and looked down. He caught his breath. Someone up on the slope above him could have gotten a clean shot at Pete on the winding road below.

But what a shot it would have been. And it would have been downhill to boot. Both the distance and the way the bullet's trajectory had to be corrected made this about the most difficult shot Slocum had ever even heard about. More than that, it had to have been made twice. The first killed the mule. The second took Pete in the head. At his finest during the war, Slocum doubted he could have made such a killing shot with such assurance. After all, two shots had brought two deaths. This sniper hit what he aimed at.

Slocum snapped his reins and let his mare set her own pace in the darkness. Traveling this road was becoming second nature to the horse now, but the sharp turns with the steep downward stretches required close attention. For an hour, Slocum and Abigail rode in silence.

Then the road widened from where he had already ridden, making for easier travel.

"I need to rest," Slocum said. If he had been in better condition, he could have ridden until his horse died under him, but he had taken too many beatings in the past few days to go on. More than that, he wanted to slow the inexorable trip down into Virginia City. If he could avoid going to the boomtown altogether, that would suit him just fine.

"Three aces," he repeated to himself. That summed up his luck for the past week and maybe longer.

"What's that, John?"

"I need to rest," he said louder. "There's a small canyon to the left with a stream coming out of it. We can water the horses, and I can rest."

"But the miners will be after us when they find you're gone."

"I have to rest," he said.

"Are you injured?"

"I can't go on much longer. Only a short time." Slocum wanted to argue Abigail out of going to Virginia City, if he could. If he couldn't, finding the first road leading away from town would be the smartest thing for him to do.

"Very well, but it's chancy," she said.

"Me falling out of the saddle's a risk I can't take either," he said. Slocum hated like hell having to drop to the ground because he barely suppressed a groan as his legs threatened to buckle under him. Somewhere, probably in the climb up from the canyon in his rescue of Pete, he had smashed his thigh into a rock. A couple days in bed would put him back in the pink, but with everybody hunting for him to drop a noose around his neck, taking time like that wasn't going to happen.

"This is a tight fit," Abigail said, riding ahead of him off the road. Her shoulders brushed the rocky sides of the crevice, but her horse kicked up water that hid any trail she might leave. Slocum followed quickly, fighting to keep his mare from rearing. Tight places bothered him, too, but there had to be a widening somewhere ahead. If not, Slocum had to figure how to back the horse out of this rocky chute.

"John!"

"What's wrong?"

"Nothing. This is incredible. I never knew such a place could exist in these barren mountains."

The crevice widened to a long, narrow canyon with enough grass growing on the floor to feed their horses for a week. A waterfall crashed into a pool at the far end of the tiny canyon.

"Just what I need," he said. He didn't have to urge his mare forward. She went directly for the edge of the pool and began drinking noisily. Slocum slipped down, supporting himself the best he could. Before he left the horse, he pawed through the saddlebags and found his six-gun and knife where Abigail had put them. He started to strap on the gun belt, then laughed ruefully.

He wanted to do nothing but sink beneath the surface of the cold mountain pool. Doing that with a six-shooter strapped around his middle was ridiculous. The gun and knife went back into the saddlebags before he took the saddle and other gear off his grateful horse.

"Are you sure this is safe?" Abigail asked as she looked around. "We're trapped here."

"Boxed in," Slocum agreed as he began stripping off his shredded clothing. He had spares in his saddlebags, but hated to use them because they were almost as tattered as what he wore. A small pile of clothing grew. He kicked off his boots and pulled off his jeans before wading into the icy water.

"That looks painful," Abigail said.

"Not the water, my bruises," he said. Slocum simply relaxed his knees and sat on the slick bottom of the pool. The water lapped around his neck while the cold sucked away his aches and pains. It wasn't as good as a bottle of whiskey, but he had to make do with what he had.

"It won't be long before they come after us," Abigail said, looking back down the narrow chasm leading to the road.

"Maybe they'll ride on past. It's still dark out," Slocum said, floating on his back and feeling the aches and pains slowly disappear. "Tracking at night's hard to do. If they use the torches, we'll see them coming as soon as they enter the crevice. Might be their horses wouldn't like the tight fit and the smoky pitch torches."

He arched his back, and saw Abigail on the bank of the

pool watching him. After a few seconds, she began unbuttoning her blouse. Every move was deliberately intended to entice him. If he had wanted, Slocum could not have pulled his eyes off the slowly revealed luscious body that came into view. She shrugged one shoulder and dropped her blouse, revealing a perfect left breast. A studied move of her right shoulder dropped the blouse down around her elbows and bared her to the waist. The sight of those fine teats caused stirrings in Slocum he had doubted were possible in his beat-up condition.

She was quite an eyeful—and she knew it.

Abigail stroked down over her hips, then worked at the fasteners on her skirt. She lithely stepped out and turned slowly. She bent over to give him a view of her perfectly shaped rump as it pressed tightly into her bloomers. Remaining bent over and facing away from him, she worked the underwear down over her hips, down her thighs, and finally past her sculpted calves.

She stayed bent over as she did a little crow hop to get free of her bloomers. Only then did she turn and begin working on her high-topped shoes. If Slocum could have grabbed a button hook, he would have ripped them open one after another. Abigail took her time, finally drawing the right shoe off to reveal her dainty foot.

He started to speak, but she pursed her ruby lips and put a finger against them, cautioning him to silence. Only when he paddled toward the center of the pool, never taking his eyes off her, did she begin work on her left shoe. By the time she was naked, Slocum was ready.

"Oh!" Abigail stuck her foot into the pool and drew back reflexively. "I didn't know it was that cold."

"Come in," Slocum urged, "and I'll slip something hot into you." He arched his back and shoved his hips up out of the water just enough to show Abigail what he meant.

"Aren't you the naughty boy," she said.

"I'm looking for a naughty girl," Slocum retorted. Abi-

gail laughed in delight and plunged into the pool, creating
a huge splash as she dived underwater. For a moment,
Slocum thought she had hit her head and was drowning.

Then she surfaced, her head between his legs. Her bright
blue eyes locked with his, then she sampled almost daintily
at his erection. Her lips brushed the tip, and her tongue
flicked back and forth like hummingbird wings teasing
him. He paddled slowly to her. She did not back away, but
let the motion thrust him deeper into her mouth. Slocum
shuddered as he felt her tongue cradling his hardness. She
began sucking and licking and giving him reason to forget
all about his sore muscles and minor scratches.

His legs draped over her shoulders while she sucked on
him, and they drifted around the pool until they came to the
waterfall. The thirty-foot plunge from higher in the mountains caused an undertow that took Slocum off the surface
and drew him underwater. Abigail followed him, her mouth
never leaving his manhood. They thrashed about and came
back to the surface under the cascading water.

Slocum got his feet under him and found the bottom so
she could stand. Abigail abandoned her post at his groin
and stood, her body pressing hotly into his. They kissed,
lost in an island of heat amid the coldness surrounding
them. Slocum felt her nipples hardening as they thrust
against his chest. His hands roamed her body, stroking over
sleek, smooth stretches of bare flesh, and finally cupping
her buttocks to hold her close. The waterfall was deafening,
but all Slocum could hear was the hammering of his own
pulse as it sped up. Abigail gripped his length and tugged
insistently.

"You promised," she shouted in his ear. "You said
you'd get something hot into me."

Slocum bent his knees and dropped. He reached both
arms between her legs, then stood. He picked her up bodily
so her thighs pressed into his upper arms, and she was bent
double where he could enter her easily. It took a few sec-

onds of jockeying, and then they both gasped as he slid deeply into her molten core.

It was awkward supporting her entire weight while she was doubled up like this, but Slocum felt a wave of strength pass through him that more than compensated for his unstable stance. He pushed his arms out a little, and then let her weight press them back to his sides. This drove her down hard around his fleshy spike so he entered her in a completely different direction than possible otherwise.

She groaned as he began moving faster. He had thought the cold would rob him of any arousal, but he was wrong. Her beauty, her tightness, her heat and desire stoked his fires. He thrust deeper and harder until Abigail cried out in release. Slocum continued for a few more seconds, and then his control vanished. He exploded in her clinging tightness and then, weak once more, sank to his knees. She floated away from him until she could get her feet on the pool bottom.

Abigail came back and knelt in front of him to kiss. He fondled her breasts and then reached around to pull her against him once more. Under the crashing water, they remained kissing and exploring each other's bodies until the last of their passions had faded.

Drifting away from beneath the waterfall, they paddled out to the center of the pool.

"You're just the medicine I needed," Slocum said. He reached over and lightly tweaked a cold-hardened nipple poking from the water.

"And you're what I needed, too, John. I've never met a man like you before. I wish we could stay here forever."

"We can for a while."

"The miners will find us."

"The marshal from town might, too, but I'm not worried. This is a safe enough place to rest up."

"It's dawn," she said. "I didn't realize it was so late—so early." She sputtered and sat up on the bottom of the pool, her breasts half hidden by the water. "You know what I mean."

"I need to get something to eat and then some rest."

"With me, there won't be any . . . resting." She reached out and caught his limp length and teased it.

"I meant sleep."

He removed her hand from his crotch and splashed out of the pool. He glanced back over his shoulder to see that she watched him with as much interest as he had watched her strip.

"When everything's squared away," he said.

"That's a promise I'll hold you to," Abigail said. "You do need to stop getting thrown in jail, though. I won't always be around to get you free."

Slocum shook like a dog and got most of the water off his body. He used his tattered clothing to dry himself, and then fished out his spare set of clothes from his saddlebags. The shirt was in worse shape than he remembered, but the jeans were an improvement over the ones he discarded.

By the time he strapped on his gun belt, Abigail was mostly dressed. He should have been slower—or more attentive. He had missed a show almost as good as her disrobing.

"What are we going to do now?" she asked.

"Where's your brother?"

"You mean William?"

He looked at her strangely.

"Of course you mean William," she went on hastily. "It's just that you distracted me so, I forgot all about him." Abigail finished buttoning her blouse and patted out wrinkles. "He went on ahead. I'm not sure where, but he was quite happy about seeing his gold mine. The Climax was exactly what he had searched for since coming to Nevada."

Slocum couldn't make heads or tails out of the Brit's curious interests.

"If he wanted me to scout for him, why'd he go on ahead?"

"Because you were locked up by the miners, that's why." Abigail realized how this sounded. She took a deep breath and then exhaled slowly. "You have to understand that William thinks of people as expendable. If you are no longer of use to him, he will push on by himself."

"I figured as much. Why are you different? Did you spend more time with your ma than he did?" Again, Slocum saw how Abigail fought to find the right words.

"Something like that. Our upbringing was so different. In many ways at least. He and I—"

Abigail stopped speaking and turned toward the crevice leading back to the road.

Slocum drew his six-shooter and cocked it, waiting for the rider to follow the sound of a horse neighing that reached their little paradise. Somebody entered the crevice out at the road. In spite of his assurances, Slocum realized they were trapped in the box canyon.

13

"John, they caught us!" Abigail grabbed his arm so hard he winced. She pressed into a large bruise that would take a week to heal properly. Slocum pulled free and pointed his pistol down the rocky crevice. Missing was impossible if he fired. The bullet might stray left or right, but the wall would cause it to ricochet directly into a rider approaching their sanctuary.

"Quiet," he said. A thousand things went through his head, but one detail always returned. The smoky torch would blind the rider and spook his mount.

"But John—"

He clamped his hand over her mouth to silence her. He watched as the outline of the rider grew less distinct from the smoke building in the crevice. And then there was nothing but a pale slash of dawn at the far end of the passageway. Only then did Slocum release the woman.

"John, how dare you touch me like that!"

"Anything you say echoes down the crevice. That would have brought them down on us in a flash."

"How'd you know they would back away?"

"We can't leave for a while," Slocum said. "I'll do a bit of the scouting your brother hired me for. Stay here." Abigail started to protest. His cold stare pinned her to the spot. He sidled into the narrow crevice and made his way to the road, marveling their horses had put up with such a tight fit going in. With the blue sky showing at the far end of the passage, the horses would have no trouble getting out. They would see sunlight and go straight for it.

He slowed and finally stopped just inside the mouth of the crevice. He pressed himself against the uphill side of the rock when another rider went past along the road, heading downhill toward Virginia City. Slocum pressed his ear to the rock and heard the steady clomp-clomp of another horse—or horses. Waiting, he counted six go by, and still he felt the vibrations that told him more traffic was on its way.

A small wagon rattled past. Standing on tiptoe allowed him to get a glimpse into the bed. He took a deep breath and then let it out. The way the canvas was tucked, that had to be Pete's body. When Bold Max rode past, Slocum knew the foreman was the final rider in the procession on its way to Virginia City for Pete's burial. Most of the miners had accompanied the corpse for a reason. Their respect for the freighter undoubtedly forced the foreman to go along with their desire to attend his funeral. It would be a send-off the likes of which the boomtown had not seen in a while. Most towns like Virginia City filled suddenly with a flood of strangers who would leave as suddenly when the gold petered out.

The men who made lasting friends were few because of the solitary nature of prospecting and mining. The crew from the Climax might be as close to a family as any of the actual families in town.

Slocum doubted they would rest easy until he was brought in for killing Pete since the freighter was one of their own.

Slocum chanced a quick look uphill and saw only dusty road. He went to the edge and peered down at the lower level where the road curled back down the mountainside, and counted a full dozen riders in addition to the pair in the wagon. He didn't bother adding in Pete. He was dead and unlikely to care if his killer was brought to justice—or if Bold Max got the wrong man.

Slocum returned to where Abigail waited anxiously.

"Well, what's going on? Tell me, John. You've got to tell me!"

He calmed her and explained, "The wagon carried Pete's body. They're probably taking him to town for burial."

"The Silver Terrace Cemetery," she said. Slocum stared at her. She looked flustered. "William and I looked around town when we passed through. We happened to stop by the town cemetery, to the north, downhill from the main part of town. You can look down on it from Main Street."

Slocum nodded. It was approaching strange that she and her brother prowled around boomtown cemeteries. William had more peculiar interests than he had shown.

"The Masons have a nice section," Abigail said lamely.

"I don't cotton much to cemeteries," Slocum said. "When my time comes, I don't figure I'll be laid to rest in one." He rubbed his neck and smiled crookedly. "The buzzards will have a feast on my bones, and that'll be the best I can hope for."

"How cynical of you," she said. "Everyone deserves a proper burial. Including that Pete person."

Something about the way she spoke put Slocum on guard.

"I want to go to his funeral," she said.

"Why's that? You didn't know him," Slocum said.

"To pay my respects, of course. Is that so odd to your Colonial ways? I should hope not." Abigail flounced away, leaving Slocum to stare at her in wonder.

"We can't go to Pete's funeral," he called after her. "The

barkeep in town thinks I killed his brother, and the Climax foreman's sure I killed Pete. If anybody spotted me, I'd be strung up before you could say Jack Robinson."

"I will not be denied this. It is only proper manners, something you are totally lacking, John Slocum," she said. She crossed her arms and glared at him.

"Bold Max might just figure out who it was that set me free. How'd you come by the key to the lock? It's not going to be hard for him to decide you and me are in cahoots. They won't hang a woman in these parts—not too often. But for someone who killed their best freighter, they might make an exception."

"Don't be ridiculous. I had nothing to do with killing this Pete person."

"I didn't either, and that didn't stop them from wanting to stretch my neck for the crime."

"I'm going. With or without you, I'm going to that funeral."

Slocum looked down at his clothing. His shirt was a different color from the one they had last seen him wearing, and his spare jeans were more faded. There wasn't a whole lot he could do about his hat because he needed to keep it pulled down low to hide his face. Anybody paying attention would spot his cross-draw holster, but he could leave that behind.

Slocum felt a cold lump forming in his gut when he realized he was thinking of walking into a cemetery filled with mourners for a man they thought he had killed—and he was coming up with ways to do it unarmed.

"Three aces," he said to himself.

"What's that?" Abigail's expression of disdain for his supposed cowardice had not changed.

"I said we ought to get on the trail or we'll miss the planting."

All the way down the mountain to Virginia City, he cursed himself for being an idiot. There was no way he could hope to strut on up to the service and not get caught. Abigail would draw a great deal of attention wherever she went because of her beauty and because the miners in a town like Virginia City already knew every unmarried female within a twenty-mile radius. The ones that weren't whores were taken as wives.

"You have to get a disguise," Slocum said as they rode past the houses at the northern end of town. The tight cluster of falling-down buildings in Virginia City was centered around the Bucket of Blood Saloon, with the Mountain of Gold, where Mac worked, at the southern end. Families populated this side of town, and that gave him a desperate idea.

"How am I supposed to do that?" Abigail asked.

"Your clothing's too nice." Slocum motioned for Abigail to remain where she was. He dismounted and went to a clothesline where a woman's dress flapped in the breeze. Stealing a woman's only other dress bothered him a mite, so he pulled it down and replaced it with a ten-dollar bill from the poke Cheswick had given him for his work.

He hurried back and tossed her the dun-colored, striped gingham dress.

"What am I supposed to do with this?" Abigail wrinkled her nose at the dress. It had been washed in lye soap strong enough to burn Slocum's fingers.

"Put it on over your clothes. Keep your head down. If you have a scarf, wear that to hide your hair. Blend in with the crowd as good as you can. Even better, stay at the back," Slocum said. "It's not like you have to go to the coffin to pay your respects."

He watched as she reluctantly pulled the dress over her clothing. She looked pleasingly plump this way, but Slocum chafed at the delay. There was no reason to go to Pete's funeral. The short time he had spent with the man had shown him to be friendly, competent, and not worth getting arrested for.

The only good thing Slocum could see about attending the service lay in nobody thinking the man accused of shooting Pete would show up.

"Let's go. Silver Terrace Cemetery is down the road."

Slocum looked over his shoulder and saw the woman who lived in the house struggling with another basket of laundry. He trotted ahead of Abigail to make sure she rode away quickly. Adding dress stealing to his long list of offenses in Virginia City wasn't something he wanted mentioned as men gathered to get drunk.

"They've begun," Abigail said. "Hurry, John. I want to see."

"You're sure you don't know where your brother is?" Slocum looked over the heads of the crowd, trying to pick out William Cheswick. If his sister was crazy as a loon about going to a funeral, he might be also.

The number turning out for Pete's funeral surprised Slocum. More than fifty people crowded through the wooden gate and trudged up the hill to a spot near the Masonic burial plots. For a moment, Slocum thought Pete was going to get planted there, but the procession passed that area, and the Fraternal Order of Moose section as well. Still, Pete had a decent enough resting place on the eastern slope of the largest hill in the graveyard. From the look of the pine coffin, someone had forked over a goodly sum to bury him in style.

"I'll wait here," Slocum said at the cemetery gate.

"Nonsense, people would stare if a woman showed up alone. They'd think there was something between Pete and me."

"Why?"

Slocum barely got the question out when he had to turn and look away. He let Abigail take his arm so he could maneuver her around to block the view of Mac and a deputy marshal with him. The two walked quickly past, never once giving Slocum a look.

"See?" Abigail said. "You're invisible. All they can think about is the funeral service. The preacher's getting ready to begin. Come along, John. Come on!" She pulled on his arm so hard, he dared not fight her or he would draw attention to himself.

The only saving grace was Abigail being camouflaged by wearing the faded dress. She melted into the crowd, and might well have been a local citizen.

Slocum dug his heels in and prevented her from getting closer to the grave. Remaining at the rear of the crowd blocked his view of the coffin, but that wasn't anything he would miss. Slocum had seen more than his share of dead men in his day. Worse, he had seen Pete when he was shot. The freighter had been about as banged up as possible before the bullet robbed him of life.

"We will have a brief viewing," the preacher said in a stentorian voice. His words carried for quite a distance, and then echoed back from the direction of Virginia City. "Pay your last respects before I begin the ceremony."

"Don't," Slocum said, but Abigail pulled free and joined the line of mourners shuffling by the now open coffin. The raised lid blocked Slocum's view, but he knew the body couldn't look very pretty. More than one of the men passing by swallowed hard and averted their eyes, confirming what Slocum knew already. No undertaker could be good enough to piece together a man's head after a bullet blasted through it. And Pete hadn't been afforded such a luxury. Bold Max had done nothing more than plunk the body into a fancy coffin for the service.

He turned when the deputy stepped in front of him, intent on getting in the line paying their respects. Slocum backed away when Mac joined the man.

"Damn shame, Pete gettin' kilt like that," the deputy said. "I always liked the son of a bitch."

"You only liked him 'cuz he bought you drinks."

The deputy snorted and nodded. "You only liked him

because he paid for all the drinks. He was a generous one, but then, them Brits spend money like water flowing through their fingers."

The two stopped talking when a commotion at the graveside caught their attention. Slocum reached for his six-shooter, but he had left it in his saddlebags. Other than the deputy, nobody at the funeral was packing iron, out of respect for the dead.

"What's goin' on?" Mac demanded.

Slocum figured it out before the barkeep. Abigail threw her hands up in the air and cried out as she tumbled backward into the preacher's arms.

"Give us room. The lady's fainted dead away. Give her some air."

A thousand things ran through Slocum's head. With the barkeep and the lawman pushing forward to Abigail's side, Slocum dared not go to her also. Turning tail and running wasn't in him, but the only way he could help her was to avoid getting thrown in the Virginia City jail again.

He walked slowly to where he had tethered the horses outside the cemetery. He'd started to mount when he heard her clarion call. "John, please!"

All eyes turned in his direction.

Even worse, the deputy's six-gun was turned in his direction, too.

"Three aces," Slocum muttered as he took his foot out of the stirrup cup and put his hands up over his head.

14

"We don't need a trial. He killed my brother. String him up now!"

"Hush, Mac. You know what the marshal says about wild talk like that," said the deputy. "We'll have a trial and you can tell your side and let him say his piece. That's what the law says."

Slocum clung to the iron bars and watched the deputy and the barkeep dancing back and forth as the argument ebbed and flowed. From what he could tell, the deputy wasn't as inclined to enforce the law as he made out. If it came down to free drinks at the Mountain of Gold Saloon or actually holding a trial, the deputy would be mighty drunk mighty fast.

"Renfro wasn't worth the powder it'd take to blow him to hell," Mac said, "but he was my blood. I'm not lettin' that sidewinder get away with killin' him over a poker game."

"I know how you feel, Mac. Me and Renfro wasn't always on the best of terms," the deputy said, "but he didn't deserve to die, even if he was cheatin' at cards again."

"He didn't cheat!"

"Now you just pipe down," the lawman said. "Ain't nobody in all of Virginia City what knows Renfro wasn't above slippin' a card or two into the deck when it suited him. Even so, killin' him was wrong."

"I'll get this trial movin' fast," Mac vowed. He left the small office, making a point of slamming the door hard behind him.

"I didn't kill him," Slocum said. "If I'd known he was a card cheat, I wouldn't have gotten into a game with him."

"Nobody asked you. I find myself agreein' more with old Mac than I ever could with a stranger," the deputy said.

"Thanks for the honesty," Slocum said bitterly. "I didn't kill him. There wasn't any money on me when Mac got the drop on me. The real killer robbed him, not me."

"I don't know about such things," the deputy said, dropping into the desk chair and hiking his feet to a comfortable angle. "That all's for a jury to ponder."

"A jury all likkered up by the dead man's brother," Slocum said.

"Makes justice go a mite faster, don't you think?" The deputy tipped his hat over his eyes, and in a few minutes was softly snoring.

Slocum knew better than to pace the cage hunting for a way out. It hadn't been here before and wouldn't be now. Sitting on the bunk, he thought hard about what he might do. His plans kept crashing to dust because he couldn't get Abigail out of his head. Why she had wanted to see the dead freighter was beyond Slocum, but fainting as she had and then calling out his name as she recovered had been the last straw. Even if he'd had his Colt Navy slung at his hip, he couldn't have shot his way out. The mourners, save for the deputy, had been unarmed. Shooting any of them would have been out of the question.

"Damn you," Slocum said harshly, and he wasn't sure who he meant. William Cheswick, Abigail, Pete, or whoever had killed Renfro. All of them. He had been in a tight spot before, but not like this. The deputy would keep a lynch mob at bay for as long as it took to open the jail door and step aside. He might not participate, but he wasn't much of a bulwark against vigilante justice.

Slocum couldn't get out, he couldn't prove his innocence, he was stuck in a cell and on his way to the gallows. Dejected, he stretched out and tried to sleep.

Somewhere around midnight, somebody banged loudly on the office door. The deputy stirred and dropped his feet to the floor. Complaining the whole way, he went to the door and opened it to a small, mousy man. Slocum peered around the corner of the door frame to get a better view, but wasn't able to see anyone else with the midnight caller. He worried about a mob coming for him, but this wasn't it.

"What do you want, Jonesy?" The deputy rubbed sleep from his eyes.

"Got a bad fight goin' on down at the Bucket. I declare, somebody's gonna get kilt if you don't break it up."

"You'd think I was the law in this town or something," the deputy said. He took a quick look in Slocum's direction and then stepped out into the night.

Slocum went wild, shaking the bars, trying to spring the lock, anything. He was as securely held as if an eagle had come down and grabbed him with its powerful talons.

He hoped that Abigail would again come rescue him, but when the door opened about ten minutes later, it was the deputy bringing in a drunk. The lawman had the miner by the scruff of the neck and the seat of his britches. He slammed him hard into the bars so he'd fall to the floor.

The deputy drew his six-gun and aimed it at Slocum. "Get on to the rear of the cell. You move a muscle and I swear, I'll drill you."

Slocum backed into the far corner as the deputy opened the cell door and kicked the miner inside. The cell door clanked shut and locked with a sound that Slocum knew had to be his death knell.

"Don't do nuthin'. I'll be back with this jasper's partner."

The deputy left again, grumbling as he went. Slocum dropped beside the drunk miner and shook him.

"They're killing your partner," Slocum said. "Then they're going to kill you."

"Wha? Who?"

"You know who," Slocum said. "The man who brought you here. He killed your partner and is bringing the dead body to torment you."

"Got torment enough," the miner said, sitting up and putting his head in his hands. "My head feels like it's gonna blow like a can of Giant blastin' powder."

"Never thought I'd hear that you let your partner die and not avenge him."

"Grogan? Grogan's dead?" Eyes slightly out of focus moved around, and finally spotted Slocum through the alcoholic haze.

"Yup. Here he is now. To taunt you with the carcass."

Slocum pointed to the office door as it slammed back against the wall from the deputy's kick. He dragged in an even burlier miner and let him fall facedown on the floor.

"You know what to do, Slocum. Get yourself to the back of the cell."

"Dead," Slocum whispered to his new cell mate. "You'll be next."

The miner stared up at the deputy but said nothing. Slocum saw how the lawman ignored the miner and kept his pistol aimed at Slocum's chest. He knew where the danger inside the cell was.

He thought he knew, but he was wrong.

The instant the cell door opened, the miner launched himself forward, falling against the deputy more than leaping at him. Strong hands clamped around the lawman's gun hand and forced the six-gun toward the floor. The deputy found himself trying to fight a drunk miner—then he had his hands full with two. Grogan had recovered enough to see the deputy fighting with his partner, and let out a roar as he charged like a wounded bull.

The deputy got caught between two husky miners and went down underneath them. Slocum stepped over the writhing pile of weakly fighting flesh and kicked the six-shooter from the deputy's hand.

"Into the cell with him or he'll be on your asses," Slocum bellowed. One of the miners obeyed by picking up the deputy and tossing him into the cell as if he were a sack of flour. He crashed into the back wall and slid down, leaving a bloody smear on the brick.

Slocum slammed the cell door and locked it.

"Hightail it or you'll spend the rest of your lives in a cage," he told the miners. They knew something had gone terribly wrong and they were part of it. They cleared out, blaming each other for whatever it was that had gotten them into this fix. Slocum rummaged through the desk, and found his Colt Navy and strapped it on. Its comforting weight made him think he could get away scot-free.

"Wha hit me?" The low groan from the jail cell warned that the deputy was coming to sooner than Slocum had expected from the whack he had taken to his head. He touched the ebony handle of his pistol, then knew he couldn't kill the lawman in cold blood. For all that he thought of the deputy, he had not been turned over to Mac for hanging. The lawman deserved some consideration for that small attention to duty.

Slocum left quickly, stepping into the cold night air. He headed for the stable and found his mare asleep in a stall. The horse turned an irritated eye on him when he hastily saddled her and led her from the stall. Vaulting into the saddle, he headed south out of town. He would have preferred to go north, but any direction out of town suited him. Somewhere north, Cheswick and Abigail must have their camp. He wanted to square things with them—and as he rode, he tried to figure out what that meant.

Abigail had been foolish wanting to see Pete's corpse. That still made no sense to him. But her brother had vanished into thin air. The base camp in the mountains where his servant probably still tended the fire and waited for his employer's return was an obvious rendezvous. But Slocum wanted to get as far away from them as he could. He still had a few dollars in his pocket to help him along his getaway trail.

Better than that, he didn't have any fatal rope burns around his neck.

The road turned eastward, and he began the long descent from high in the mountains. Virginia City had not proved to be his kind of town after all, but then no town was. He got along better living off the land a hundred miles from the nearest human.

By dawn, he was too tired to go on. His mare began faltering, and this convinced him to rest. He had put only a few miles between him and the gallows, but it would have to do.

He dismounted and let the mare graze at some grass alongside the road. Barely had he spread his bedroll when he heard approaching hoofbeats. Slocum grabbed for his Winchester, then slid it back into its saddle sheath. The rider came from the east, not from Virginia City.

He flopped down and put his hands under his head so he could watch the road. With luck, the rider would pass by and never spot him. It was too late for him to get out of sight, so luck on his part and inattention of the early morning rider had to do.

The rider was not inattentive, and Slocum still had no good luck.

"Howdy, mister," the rider called. He hooked his leg around the pommel and leaned forward. "You got any coffee brewing for a tired pilgrim?"

"Nope, don't," Slocum said. He sat up and moved to get his hand closer to his six-shooter.

"Well, sir, if you'll get a fire going, I'll share my coffee with you. How're you fixed for food?"

"I'm all right in that regard," Slocum said. He had supplies left from Cheswick's camp, but what he wanted most of all was for the rider to ignore him. If the man continued to Virginia City and happened to be questioned by the deputy, a posse with fresh horses would be on this road in nothing flat.

"You're lucky, getting a good night's sleep," the man said. He stepped down and began working through his saddlebags for coffee. "Me, I been ridin' all the livelong night. I'm so tired, I'm close to fallin' over asleep."

"Do tell." Slocum gathered firewood and made a small pit. The man watched him closely.

"You spend the night?"

Slocum nodded as he scraped away dirt to make a pit deep enough to hold his firewood.

"Come from Virginia City?"

"Not much else along this road," Slocum said. He got out his box of lucifers and started a fire. He fed in small twigs and got them hot enough to ignite larger ones. Soon, he had a decent fire blazing that would boil coffee.

"You didn't have a fire last night when you stopped?"

"Is that all you do? Ask questions?" Slocum looked up and saw the man's coat pulled back to reveal a star.

"It's one of the hazards of my job, I reckon. I'm Ethan Dinks, marshal up in Virginia City. I've been huntin' for a renegade Injun."

"You didn't find him," Slocum said.

"Not unless I got me an invisible prisoner," Dinks said. He chuckled. "I declare, he might as well have been invisible out on the trail. Best damn woodsman I ever encountered."

"Paiute?"

"You must be headin' south from way up north," Dinks said. "We got a half dozen bands of Northern Paiutes kickin' up their heels and feelin' their oats."

"Saw some," Slocum said since this was a safe enough topic. "They had women with them but I didn't see any children."

"They're always on the move. Entire villages pull up stakes and move. Damn hard keepin' track of where they're goin'." The marshal put his coffeepot on the fire, filled it with water from his canteen, and then tossed in coffee. "Need a few eggshells in the pot to keep it from gettin' too bitter. You ever try that?"

"Still tastes bitter if the coffee's boiled too long," Slocum allowed.

"True," Dinks said. They sat in silence as the coffee brewed. Slocum held out his tin cup for the marshal to pour. He was feeling relaxed now. The marshal would find out soon enough about the trouble in his town, but by then Slocum could be another dozen miles down the road. If he spotted a likely area, he'd leave the road and cut across country. In such mountainous terrain, tracking him would be nigh on impossible.

"You make good coffee, Marshal."

"I tell you, I need this. Otherwise, I'd have to prop open my eyelids with toothpicks." The marshal downed his coffee and poured himself a second cup. "What's your business?"

"Looking for a job tending cattle," Slocum said.

"You might go on into Virginia City. There're a couple spreads in the area what supply beeves to the miners. One owner's a friend of mine. I could put in a word for you."

"That's mighty neighborly, Marshal," Slocum said, "but the cold's getting to me. I'm headed for warmer, lower country."

"Get far enough south and you'll wish you were back where it isn't a hundred degrees in the day and zero at night. The south desert's a man killer."

"I'll take my chances. Arizona is more to my liking now anyway."

"Wish you luck," the marshal said. He tossed the dregs of his coffee into the fire, stood, and drew his six-shooter before Slocum realized what was happening. "I think it might be a better idea if you and me moseyed on back to town just for a spell."

"What's going on?" Slocum judged his chances of throwing down against a veteran lawman who had his six-shooter pointed squarely at his chest. From the steady grip and the steely look, Slocum realized his chances were zero.

"Now, that's what I want to figure out. You camped for the night, but it looks from your lathered horse that you just arrived not long 'fore me. You certainly didn't fix any food. No matter how tired a man gets on the trail, food's a consideration. And if you'd spent the night with only that thin blanket, you'd have built a fire or froze."

"You're jumping to some wild conclusions."

"You just might be right. If you are and nothing's amiss in Virginia City, I'll apologize, buy you a decent meal, and put you up in the finest hotel in town." The marshal gestured for Slocum to pack up his gear and mount. "And if I'm not, well, then, I can offer you lodging in my jail."

Slocum knew all about those accommodations.

15

"Bugger me cross-eyed, look at what the marshal's bringin' back!"

Slocum glowered at the mousy man the deputy had called Jonesy. He sat outside the jailhouse, cleaning his fingernails with a short knife, but seeing Dinks riding in with a prisoner brought him to his feet.

The outcry brought half the town running, or so it seemed. They all talked at once, making the marshal scowl.

"Hush up, y'all," Dinks bellowed. "What the hell's goin' on?"

"Why, Marshal, you brung back the varmint that killed Renfro and Pete—you know Pete? The freighter fella. You brung back an escaped prisoner, and we didn't even know you was on the trail!"

"Escaped?" Ethan Dinks looked hard at Slocum. "You escaped from my jail?"

Slocum said nothing. By this time, the deputy had come running and skidded to a halt a few feet away. He had his six-gun out and pointed at Slocum's head.

"You caught him, Marshal! I thought he was gone for good. He bashed in my skull and got away."

"You had him?"

"Me and Mac, we caught him at Pete's funeral. He was there to gloat over what he'd done. He blowed half of Pete's fool head off!"

The crowd all began shouting at once. Dinks put his fingers in his mouth and cut through the din with an ear-piercing whistle.

"Pete's dead? And Renfro?"

"He's the one what done it, Marshal," explained Jonesy. He pointed his skinny knife at Slocum and said, "We knows he's guilty 'cuz he ran."

"You do what they say?" Before Slocum could answer, Dinks shook his head and said, "No, of course you didn't. Nobody's ever guilty of any damn thing in this town. Clear the way. I want him locked up and I want you and you," he said, pointing at his deputy and Jonesy, "inside right now."

"What about me, Marshal? Renfro was my brother."

"Why not? The more the merrier. But the office'll be crowded with all of you. The rest of you gawkers, git!"

Slocum was hauled down by the deputy and Mac and dragged back inside the jailhouse. Before the marshal came in and flopped down in his chair, Slocum was securely locked up again.

"He's in and out of this here jail more than you are, Marshal," Jonesy said. "This is the third time he's been locked up. Got away the other two times."

"How?"

For a moment, not one of them spoke. Then Mac filled the silence gruffly. "He's got accomplices. That's the only explanation."

"Who?"

The marshal rocked back and waited. Mac and the deputy looked a little panicked. Then Mac went on. "Don't know, but he has to have one. When we caught him after he gunned down my brother, he didn't have any money on him."

"Why not?" Dinks called to Slocum.

"Renfro wiped me out in the poker game. He was already dead and robbed when I saw him."

"Your gun'd been fired!"

"I shot at whoever robbed him," Slocum said.

"So?" Dinks looked hard at Mac.

"He's covering for somebody, that's what he's doin'. His partner got the money. That's why we didn't find it on him."

"Mac's got a theory. You deny it's possible?"

"That's not what happened," Slocum said. "Not that any of you are likely to listen."

"That's a fact," Dinks said. "You're charged with murderin' Renfro Macallister. It's up to a jury to decide if you done it. Now what's this about Pete?"

"He killed him, too," blurted Jonesy. "He was ridin' alongside Pete, goin' up the hill to the Climax. He shot him down like a dog!"

"So?" The marshal looked back at Slocum.

"I was riding with him. Somebody shot the mule and we went over the side of the road in the wagon. I helped Pete back up. He had a busted leg, but when he stood up on his good leg, somebody shot him from way off."

"How far's that?"

Slocum considered the range from what he had seen when he had escaped the dynamite shed at the mine. He hadn't realized what he was claiming until now.

"Five hundred yards."

"So somebody shot the mule, then shot Pete, and did it with two shots from a quarter mile? That's mighty fine shootin', don't you agree?"

Slocum stayed silent. During the war when he had served as a sniper, such a shot would have been more luck than skill. The wind, the downward angle of the shot, the sheer audacity of the deed made it seem impossible—and Slocum had witnessed it.

"Either you're one hell of a liar or it really happened. Which is it? No, don't answer me. The jury'll decide that as well.

"Anything else been goin' on while I've been gone?" Dinks directed this at his deputy. The man launched into a litany of petty crimes. Slocum saw that the marshal hardly paid attention. These were the ordinary misdemeanors that filled any lawman's time in a boomtown. Drunkenness, fights, horse thieving, these were the time wasters. But he'd left town, and had had two murders to come back to.

"All right, you fellas git. I need to do some thinkin'."

"When's the trial gonna be?" demanded Mac. "I kin get six men together by noon."

"We need a judge. Old Man Larousse is out riding circuit and ought to be through in a week or so. Unless you're right about him havin' an accomplice, he's stayin' locked up this time."

"Judge Larousse is senile," protested Mac. "He don't know what day it is, much less the letter of the law."

"He's what we have to work with. He convicted the Purdy boys, didn't he? Now I told you to clear out and let me be."

Jonesy didn't go far. Slocum saw him hunker down outside the door to wait for an errand to run or a murderer to turn in. The deputy and Mac left together, heading in the direction of the Mountain of Gold.

"If Mac gets enough of his customers drunk, they'll come for me," Slocum said.

"That's possible," Dinks said. "But it ain't gonna happen while I'm marshal of Virginia City. I put on the badge a month ago, and I intend to wear it for a good, long time."

"That's a most admirable ambition, Marshal," said a cultured British voice. Slocum moved to the other side of the cell to get a look at a tall, rail-thin man with a walrus mustache touched with gray who was just outside the jail. He stepped in, took off a bowler hat, and brushed it off with his elbow. Slocum wasn't sure what the material was in the man's spotless jacket, but it might have been English tweed. He wore calf-high riding boots that had once been polished like mirrors, but now needed some buffing. A gold watch chain dangled from a vest pocket, and he carried a silver-tipped walking stick.

"Who might you be?"

"I, sir, am another practitioner of our craft."

"What's that?"

"Law enforcement. I am Lionel Partridge, chief inspector, Scotland Yard." He bowed just the slightest amount. Steel gray eyes fixed on the marshal and never wavered.

"Do tell. What brings a law officer such as yourself out to the American frontier?"

"Murder, sir. I am on the track of a vicious murderer."

"Well, if that's the one you mean, you'll have to wait your turn." Marshal Dinks jerked his thumb in Slocum's direction.

"You are quite mistaken about him, Marshal. I have followed him for some time and vouch for his innocence."

"In which killing?"

"Both, sir. I saw him emerge from the Mountain of Gold drinking establishment at the precise instant your Renfro Macallister was being robbed. It was at this time that Mr. Slocum came upon the perfidy, fired, and missed. The robber fired back at Mr. Slocum, then shot and killed his victim and escaped."

"So what was you doin' all that time, Mr. Partridge?"

"Chief Inspector Partridge, if you please, sir. I was on the trail of the actual killer. Percival Cheswick is wanted for the murder of his older brother, Ralph, in England."

"And this Percival fellow killed Renfro? Why?"

"For sport, no doubt," Partridge said. "He is remorseless."

"And the killing up at the mine road?"

"As I stated succinctly, sir, I have followed Mr. Slocum for some time. I witnessed the first shot that killed the lead mule. The shot came from the area he indicated. I was on my way to apprehend Percival when the second shot was fired, this one killing the wagon driver."

"You don't know who fired the shot since you didn't see it," Dinks said.

"The killing shot was fired from the top of the rise. Mr. Slocum was with the murder victim. No other shot was fired."

"All this will come out in a trial, I suppose," Dinks said. "That's assumin' you'd be willin' and able to testify under oath."

"I would consider it a boon, sir, if you released Mr. Slocum. His frontier skills are extraordinary. With his aid, I am sure I can bring Percival Cheswick to justice in a nonce."

"I can't up and let him go on your say-so. You might be who you claim. Then again, you might be his accomplice, the one Mac was goin' on about."

"Contact Scotland Yard to verify my identity. I know you have a telegraph office here. I have used it to contact my superiors in London."

"Even if you're who you say you are, and I'm not callin' you a liar, I can't let him go 'fore he stands trial."

"I see," Partridge said. "This is quite a pity since I require his inestimable services. I find myself quite at a loss to perform the scouting required to bring Percival Cheswick to justice."

Slocum blinked and almost missed what happened as Lionel Partridge spoke. If he had been lulled into not thinking the Brit was a menace, the marshal was doubly caught unawares. Partridge swung his cane and clipped Dinks on the side of the head. The marshal looked surprised. Then he looked unconscious.

"This is quite irregular, old chap," Partridge said, "but the frontier brings out such devil-may-care in me."

"He'll think you're the one who robbed Renfro."

"Nothing stands in the way of duty, Mr. Slocum." The way he spoke in such a solemn tone, Slocum had to believe him.

"Folks in these parts have hard heads," Slocum said, remembering how the deputy had recovered so fast after having his head smashed into a wall. "We had better hightail it out of town."

"I took the liberty of preparing your steed. She awaits outside," said Partridge as he tossed Slocum the keys to the cell.

Slocum once more let himself out, then grabbed his six-shooter and holster, aware of how Partridge was studying him so closely.

"Where do we head?" Slocum asked as he stepped outside. The cold wind blowing off the higher elevations chilled him to the bone, but the sense of freedom kept him from minding. His freedom would evaporate once Marshal Dinks got a posse together. Not only Mac but the peace officer would follow him to the ends of the earth. Even going back to London with Lionel Partridge would not get him far enough away to be forgotten.

"I rather thought you would lead the way, Mr. Slocum," the detective said. "My wanderings about have not turned up evidence of Percival Cheswick at all."

"You were following William hoping he would lead you to Percival?"

"Yes, quite. The whole while I did not catch even a glimpse of Percival. It led me to believe his younger brother knew nothing of his whereabouts. I had decided to approach William when you showed up in town and became embroiled in that nasty business with the barman's brother."

"I have no idea where to begin hunting for this Percival

Cheswick," Slocum admitted. "What made you think he was around here, other than following William?"

"I learned that a man who resembled Percival had been seen at the mining camp. I thought he might be a miner, but Percival was, after all, of noble birth. Such an occupation would never suit him."

"Who owns the mine? Might be he put up the money to develop it."

"How would that be possible?"

Slocum rode north and found the road leading up the mountainside to the Climax Mine. For such a short stretch of rocky road, this held a considerable amount of memory for him. Not only had Pete been killed on the way to the summit, but Slocum and Abigail had spent an enjoyable few hours at the far end of a crevice under a waterfall. Slocum said nothing about this to Partridge as they made their way up the steep slope.

"Prospectors find the gold, but they're cantankerous coots," Slocum said. "Most aren't suited to working a claim. They'd rather sell and move on to get the thrill of finding another strike than staying and getting rich."

From the expression on Partridge's thin face, Slocum knew the detective found this difficult to believe. However, Slocum had seen it time and again. Prospectors preferred solitude. Working a mine required interaction with dozens of others, in the mill, in town, with shippers and bankers and others who would intrude on their privacy. Better to take a few dollars for what might be the mother lode and move on than to remain tied down to a hole in the ground.

"So you are saying Percival Cheswick might have purchased the Climax from some prospector? I say, he hardly had any money. That is the motive for him murdering his elder brother. Lord Ralph held the extensive Northumbrian family estate and monies rather tightly."

"It's a guess. I never saw the owner. The foreman can tell us about the real owner, but you'll have to do the talking."

"Ah, yes, Bold Max Carson," Partridge said. "A man of few words but infinite action. However did you escape when he locked you in that rather sturdy shed?"

Slocum didn't want to go into his relationship with yet another of the Cheswick siblings and shrugged it off.

"You are a resourceful rogue, Mr. Slocum. It is a pleasure riding with you rather than after you."

Slocum kept looking down the winding road to see if the marshal had sent a posse after them yet. He expressed his concern to Partridge.

"The marshal will be rather quiet about it, I suspect," Partridge said. "After the accolades he received when he arrived with you in custody, and the heap that he piled on the heads of those who permitted you to evade custody, it is not going to be pleasant admitting that he allowed you to escape."

"Might be," Slocum allowed. "But if his pride is bruised enough, he'll have everybody in Virginia City on our trail."

"So far, not so," Partridge said.

They rode hard, and Slocum's mare was wobbling along when they got within a hundred yards of the mouth to the Climax Mine.

"I'll see about the owner," Partridge said, giving Slocum a hard look. Then the British detective rode to the mine, dismounted, and disappeared inside.

Slocum knew this was his chance to get away. Keep riding down the back road to the valley, and from there he could disappear into the wilderness of the Sierra Nevada Mountains. There was no reason to help the Scotland Yard detective. None.

Slocum snapped the reins to get his horse to the back road.

16

Slocum rode less than a hundred yards before he began thinking up excuses not to ride away from the detective. His mare was too tired. Partridge would be able to see him on a lower level of the road and either stop him or set Bold Max's miners on his trail. There were a lot of other excuses, but it came down to something far simpler than any of them. Slocum owed Lionel Partridge, and he always paid his debts.

Drawing rein, he waited in shadows where he wasn't as likely to be seen by a miner not working deep inside the Climax. He turned everything he knew over and over in his head, and things simply did not fit together right. Before he could figure out what was wrong, he heard a horse coming down the trail.

"There you are, old chap. I spoke at length with the foreman, and he dissuaded me of any notion that Percival Cheswick owns this mine. The owner lives in San Francisco, is from Michigan, and is about a hundred years of age, if Bold Max's estimate is accurate, and wheezed like a fireplace bellows the one time he inspected the property."

"What do we do now?"

"Bold Max did identify this sketch of Percival I showed him, though." Partridge pulled a many-times-folded piece of paper from an inner pocket and held it up for Slocum to examine. "Do you recognize him?"

"Can't say that I do," Slocum said.

"I was of the same opinion, but Bold Max, man of few words that he is, sounded quite adamant about his identification."

"So where do we ride?"

Slocum didn't like what Lionel Partridge told him. When he found out what they had to do once they got there, he was even more inclined to curse himself as a fool for not riding off when he had the chance.

"You Yanks are not superstitious, are you?"

"I'm not a Yankee," Slocum said with some venom. He couldn't care less what Partridge called him, but he had to vent his bile somehow.

"The moon will rise in another hour. Should we begin?"

"Go to hell," Slocum grumbled. He picked up the shovel, pushed open the wooden gate leading into Silver Terrace Cemetery, and hiked up the steep hill to the fresh grave. The recent burial made for easier digging. Another week or two and the dirt would have settled in, baked in the sun, and been as hard as rock to dig.

"You are a splendid sport, Mr. Slocum," Partridge said. "I knew there was a reason I spirited you away from the marshal."

"Grave robbing might be worse than murder," Slocum said.

"Oh, quite. In England earlier this century, we had quite the spate of grave robbers. All dug up the corpses for experiments and medical schools, they said, but Scotland Yard records show many performed quite vile sexual acts on the bodies."

Slocum's shovel hit the top of the pine box. He looked around to be sure the sound hadn't carried in the still night air. The only other living soul around stared down into the grave with some expectation. Slocum wasn't going to disappoint Partridge by stopping now. He dug like a prairie dog for another few minutes, dirt flying back in a steady cloud, then threw down his shovel and said, "Go on. This is your show now."

"I suppose it is," Lionel Partridge said. He jumped in, dropped to one knee, worked the sharp tip of his walking stick under the nailed-on lid, and applied leverage. The nails screeched like banshees as they were pulled from the wood. When the lid popped off, Slocum jumped in spite of himself.

"That's Pete. The freighter I was supposed to have murdered."

"So I see," Partridge said, using his stick to push back the bandage covering half the dead man's face.

Slocum saw the empty eye socket and the scarred face, but he also saw a resemblance he had never noticed before.

"That could be William Cheswick," he said.

"Rather, it is Percival." The detective held his drawing next to Pete's face and compared the bone structure and other features. "It would seem he came to America and found a job that suited his wild spirit."

"He said he rode the steeplechase, whatever that is," Slocum said. "He was good with animals, and that's how he got a job driving freight."

"Yes, definitely Percival." Partridge shook his head. "I had so wanted to take him back to the gallows for the vile murder of his brother."

"If he's dead and his older brother is, too, does William inherit everything?"

"So it would seem, Mr. Slocum. Do close him back up. We have more traveling to do, in which you can be of most estimable aid."

"Finding William Cheswick," Slocum said. He refitted the coffin lid and then shoveled dirt back on top of Pete— Percival Cheswick. He understood why the man had changed his name. Being called Percy would have made him the butt of jokes wherever he went. Pete was a solid name that miners and cowboys could chew on for a while, deciding they liked the way it rolled off their tongues.

As he worked, Slocum thought on how Abigail had fainted at the sight of the body. She might have had an inkling who was being buried that day, but seeing her older brother all laid out the way he was had to be a shock. He just wished she hadn't made such a fuss drawing attention to herself. When she had called out to him, there wasn't any way the deputy or Mac could have overlooked him.

"There," Slocum said, tamping the last of the dirt down. "Think he can rest in peace now?"

"Not until his murderer is brought to justice," Partridge said. "It will be my life's mission to see that accomplished."

Slocum reached for his six-shooter when he heard a rattling buggy going by the cemetery. He stood stock-still and watched as it continued down the hill to a small knot of houses at the bottom. Living with a cemetery above you had to be nerve-wracking. More than once, Slocum had seen flash floods wash coffins downhill.

"You are understandably nervous," Partridge said. He put his arm around Slocum's shoulders and steered him from the graveyard and the work he had done there. "This business will soon be at an end for you. Where do we look for William?"

Slocum had a few ideas.

"I say, Mr. Slocum, we have been on the hunt for a solid week and seem no closer to finding him. Are you sure you know what he is up to?"

Lionel Partridge always spoke in a roundabout fashion.

Slocum knew he was questioning his scout's ability to find
the trail. After retracing their way across the mountain and
avoiding the miners at the Climax, they had ridden criss-
cross fashion hunting for any trace of William Cheswick's
camp. Where he had been camped in the canyon gave no
hint of his destination. The fire pits had been cold and un-
used for days, and whatever equipment had been left behind could be accounted for by having most of his servants
hightail it after the Paiute attack.

"He wanted to hunt bear," Slocum said. "The best spot
for that is to the north, higher in the mountains. Without a
guide, though, he might have gone in any direction."

"That's why we roam endlessly back and forth hunting
for spoor?"

"Something like that," Slocum said. "I'm also making
sure we're the only ones out here hunting for him."

"A posse from town?"

"The Indians," Slocum corrected. He watched his back
trail constantly for any trace of Marshal Dinks and his deputy, but the Paiutes were a dangerous element in the area.
After all they had been through, with Cheswick stealing
away one of their women and Slocum dispatching a war
chief, they would kill first and never ask questions.

"I saw the aborigines, but only from a distance."

"You were poking about a long time. Why didn't you
meet up with Cheswick earlier?"

"William? Well," Partridge said slowly, "I wanted to see
if he met his brother. Letting William do my work appealed
to me."

"You're a fish out of water in these parts," Slocum said.
"How'd your superiors ever come to send you after Percival?"

"There is a matter of a protracted vacation," Partridge
said.

"So Ralph's murder stuck in your craw, and you had to
bring in the man responsible?"

"Something like that." Partridge thought for a moment and then said, "Ralph was a dear friend. When he was poisoned, I ascribed it to his wanton ways. Then it became clear that the poisoning was deliberate. Arsenic introduced slowly is undetectable until death claims its victim. I recognized the symptoms, but too late."

Slocum nodded as he began to understand. Ralph Cheswick might have been a friend, but Partridge blamed himself for the death because he had not prevented it. His superiors probably thought the killer was beyond their jurisdiction, but Lionel Partridge had made it a matter of personal honor to bring some justice to the case.

"What's that ahead?" Partridge pointed to a thin column of smoke snaking its way into the sky. Slocum had missed it because the leaden storm clouds forming over the mountains were the same color.

"You've got sharp eyes," Slocum said. He took a deep whiff of the air and caught nothing but the scent of rain. "We'll have to hurry to beat the storm."

As he spoke, a jagged bolt of lightning seared downward and touched a mountaintop beyond where the smoke rose.

"How do we know it's Cheswick?"

"We don't," Slocum said. "I'll scout ahead and be sure. As you said, we don't want to run afoul of more Indians."

As they rode, the first heavy drops of a summer storm began splattering on them. Slocum pulled his hat down, and quickly discovered the bullet hole in the brim let water trickle down on his shoulder as surely as if he had built in a drain spout. He got them across a dry riverbed only minutes before a loud roar echoed throughout the valley and a wall of water rushed past.

"That would never do to cross," Partridge said, watching the churning, roiling stream. "Rivers in England are somewhat better behaved."

"Ever so proper," Slocum said, smiling. "Flash floods

are a constant worry in the mountains. We'd better find shelter and let this blow over." He pulled up his collar to the increasingly hard rain.

"If we reach Cheswick's camp, we can ride out the storm in style. He had a rather fine tent," said Partridge.

Slocum considered the matter and finally agreed. He would have preferred a cave on higher ground out of the valley and the rain, but Partridge was right. By the time Slocum found such a cave, the shower might be over and they'd be wet. If it didn't let up any time soon, being in a tent would let them stay drier—and they'd have found Cheswick.

Head down against the rising wind, Slocum rode on until he found a muddy game trail. If Cheswick had come this way, he would have followed the path because it was easier than fighting his way through the undergrowth in the increasingly dense forest around them.

The rain pattered down on leaves high above and robbed the storm of some of its fury, but Slocum found himself constantly assaulted by water dripping from above. His horse shied when thunder crackled behind them.

"Sure you want to push on?" He had to shout at Partridge to make himself heard over the rain.

"I am not used to such weather. London fog is one thing, but this is a terrible squall."

"Stay on the leeward side of a big tree," Slocum advised. "With so many trees around, it's not likely the one you pick'll be struck by lightning."

"That's reassuring," Partridge said. "That tree? Is it a good one?"

"As good as any," Slocum said. Partridge had decided on a maple tree, sturdy and not likely to be struck since it was shorter than surrounding loblolly pines. "I'll scout ahead and be back in a half hour at the outside."

"Do." Partridge shivered and pulled his coat around him.

Slocum made certain he could locate the detective again, and pressed on at a quicker clip. The game trail was a small river of its own now, obliterating any recent hoofprints, but Slocum felt he was getting near. He suddenly emerged from the dense growth and looked across a clearing at Cheswick's red, white, and blue tent flapping and snapping in the wind. The fire pit in front was long since inundated by the heavy rain. Slocum put his heels to the mare's flanks and trotted over.

"Hello!"

When he didn't get an answer, he dismounted, poked his head into the tent, and looked around.

It was empty.

17

Slocum searched the tent for some sign where the occupants had gone. Nothing had been unpacked. Trunks and other cases were neatly lined up along one tent wall, now flapping furiously as the wind mounted. He ducked back into the storm and hunted for Quinton. The servant had brought all this to the tent. Where had he gone?

Slocum did what he could to find tracks, but the increasingly heavy rain efficiently blotted out anything he might have found on the ground. Every step he took caused him to sink up to his ankles in mud. A quick circuit of the camp revealed nothing he hadn't already discovered in the tent.

That meant he had nothing. William Cheswick and his servant were gone. Slocum took a deep breath and let it out. Abigail Cheswick was missing, too. He hadn't seen her since Pete's—Percival's—funeral.

He stepped up into the saddle and retraced his path to where he found Lionel Partridge hunkered down, coat pulled up over his head and getting wetter by the minute.

"Is it the right campsite?" the detective called against the rising howl of the wind.

"You're the detective. Come on and tell me what happened."

"Blimey, this is foul weather." As Partridge stood, a gust of wind almost knocked him off his feet. Slocum realized that the Scotland Yard detective was frailer and older than he had first thought. The iron gray in his walrus mustache had been earned through long years of life. The wind and rain plastered the Brit's coat and pants against a frame that was close to being emaciated.

"Hurry up. You need help?"

"I say, Mr. Slocum, I am quite capable of mounting by myself." In spite of his boast, Partridge struggled to get into the saddle. They rode back to the camp, where Slocum pointed out how isolated it was. He let Partridge discover the desolation within.

"What happened, eh? Yes, you are right. This calls for a good detective. It's lucky there is one handy," Partridge said, chuckling to himself. He walked around the tent, examining the trunks and boxes, and finally returned to the center of the tent, stroking his mustache as he thought.

"You see what you needed to see?" Slocum asked.

"Eh? Why, yes. What is it?"

Slocum led both horses into the tent. It became more crowded, but leaving them out in the storm was criminal. He tethered them to a trunk and then tended the pair the best he could. All the while, Partridge stood in the middle of the tent with a far-off expression on his face. When Slocum finished, the detective pointed to the tent flap where they had entered.

"Did you notice that, Mr. Slocum? The sure sign of foul play?"

Slocum examined the canvas and saw red smudges. Rubbing his finger over them caused a smear. He had barely noticed it before, thinking it was dye running from the colorful canvas.

"Blood?"

"Quite so," Partridge affirmed. "There was a fight here. You can barely detect the traces, but more blood pooled near the door. If it was not raining, I am certain we could follow a trail of blood away and find who was the victim."

"There're only the three," Slocum said. He reached out as if to grab the bloody spot on the canvas. "It might be Abigail's blood. Or Quinton's. From the angle of the stain and the height, I'd say it was put there by someone considerably shorter than Cheswick."

"Capital, Mr. Slocum. You would make a fine Yard detective."

"To take your job? Did you retire or did they fire you?"

Lionel Partridge stared at him for a moment, his eyes desolate. His mustache twitched and then he said softly, "I was retired against my wishes."

"Health reasons? You're wasting away, though under those clothes it's hard to tell."

"Yes, you would make a fine detective. I am pursuing Ralph Cheswick's murderer as a capstone to my otherwise undistinguished career. My cases were trivial until he was found dead. Not only was he my friend, he will be my legacy."

"If I had to make a guess, I'd say it was Quinton's blood. The thickness of the fingers on the canvas make that more likely."

"Yes, of course," Partridge said. He unfolded a camp stool and sank onto it in the middle of the tent. "I am at a loss to discern how it came that the servant was injured."

The storm blew through the tent flap and chilled Slocum. He fastened the ties on the flap to hold back some of the elements. As he worked against the wind, he tried to piece together everything that might have happened. Not enough information. He could track with the best, but he needed a trail. Otherwise, he wandered in circles.

"I'll hunt for whoever's wounded."

"When the storm abates, of course," Partridge said. "It is turning beastly out there."

"A mountain storm can last for a few minutes or it might rage for days. Since this one's been going for an hour or more, there's not likely to be an end in sight soon," Slocum said. "Stay here."

Over Partridge's protests, he opened the tent flap, and was swallowed by the storm within seconds. The wind blew the raindrops until they were almost parallel with the ground.

If he was injured and came out of the tent, he would head directly away to reach the nearest trees. Bracing against the wind, he made his way across the barren stretch of grass, and finally got to a trio of junipers, each vying for survival by outgrowing the other two. The rain had washed away real proof, but he thought he saw blood in the bark. He stepped around the trees and was shielded a little from the storm.

Directly ahead lay Quinton, facedown on the carpet of pine and juniper needles. A flash of lightning lit up the area, giving Slocum warning of what he would find when he rolled Quinton over. The servant was dead. Pulling open his jacket, Slocum found a bullet wound in the middle of his chest.

Slocum grabbed Quinton's arms and pulled him to a sitting position, then hefted him over his shoulder. Staggering under the weight and the increasing wind and rain, Slocum made his way back to the tent. He stopped a few yards away when he saw shadows moving across one canvas wall. With a grunt, he dropped Quinton's body and drew his six-shooter.

As he pushed aside the flap and covered the men inside, he relaxed. Partridge sat in a chair across from William Cheswick. Both sipped at something from china cups.

"Come in, Slocum. It's good to meet someone from the home country," Cheswick said. "Spot of tea? I'm afraid it is not brewed properly. Quinton got off and I don't know where."

Slocum looked at Partridge, wondering what the Scotland Yard detective had told Cheswick.

"I haven't gotten to that yet," Partridge said, as if reading Slocum's mind. He didn't have to be that astute. He saw the question on Slocum's face. What he couldn't read was that Quinton was dead with a bullet in his heart.

"What's that, Mr. Partridge?" Cheswick asked.

Slocum took the question to mean that Partridge had neglected to mention he was a detective after Cheswick's brother.

"I am a . . . solicitor with sad news. I have come to this wilderness to find your brother to inform him that your elder brother, Ralph, has perished."

Slocum settled down on a crate and tucked his six-shooter into its holster while he waited to see Cheswick's reaction. The man's face was perfectly illuminated by a small coal oil lamp set on the floor between the men. Somehow, Cheswick had heated enough water to make his abominable tea using that same lamp's flame.

"I suspected Percy was here myself," said Cheswick. "He left for America as Ralph took ill. After Ralph's funeral, I came to this wilderness in part to find him and tell him the news."

"I have further bad news," said Partridge. "Percival also has died."

Cheswick's expression flickered from fear to . . . what? Slocum couldn't put a name to it. The man's eyes turned blank and all the facial muscles locked into place, none so much as twitching.

"What happened to Percy?"

"It was murder, I am sorry to say. He was shot."

Again, Slocum saw the play of emotion on the man's face. Cheswick tried to hide it. His eyes left Partridge and fixed on Slocum, as if he realized anything he said or did now would put him in danger.

"You're the only surviving heir, aren't you?" Slocum

asked. "That's makes you lord high muckety-muck of Northumberland."

"That's hardly the title, but it would seem to be accurate. Dammit, where's Quinton? Quinton!"

"Where's Abigail?" Slocum asked.

"Oh, bother. What does that matter?" Cheswick made a shooing motion with his hand, as if brushing Slocum off. "I want my servant to brew proper tea for my guest. It's not often I have a visitor from so close to home. Really, Mr. Partridge, I must hear all the news."

The news of Percival's death had not fazed Cheswick. If anything, a flicker of amusement had come to his lips when Partridge announced Percival's murder. William knew Percival and Ralph were both dead and that he was now immensely wealthy instead of being a ne'er-do-well bumming around the West, kidnaping Indian squaws and shooting wild animals for sport.

Slocum thought a moment more, this time about how Partridge had presented the information to Cheswick. He had not declared himself to be a detective and nothing had been said about arresting Percival—Pete—if he had gotten to him before someone put a bullet through his head.

"Mind if I go outside and look around?" Slocum asked.

"Go, go," Cheswick said irritably, but Slocum looked to the detective for permission. He wasn't going to leave Partridge alone with a man who just might have murdered his brother. From all Slocum could tell, he might have murdered both brothers to get their inheritance. A wink from Partridge freed Slocum from having to stand guard over him. The detective had experience dealing with criminals and knew the British mind.

If anything, the rain pelted down even harder as Slocum stepped into the storm. He dragged Quinton's body away from the tent and left it under a nearby scrub oak that provided no protection but that made Slocum feel he was doing something for the dead man. Slocum wondered where

Abigail had gone, and worried about her. Her brother might be pruning the family tree and, having done with his brothers, might consider her to be next, though Slocum couldn't see why since the law of primogeniture kept her from ever inheriting the family fortune.

He prowled around in the rain but saw nothing. Hunkering down against a big-boled tree to think, he decided that Abigail wouldn't be far if her brother had tried to kill her. There was nowhere for her to flee. With this thought in mind, Slocum stood and walked out into the clearing and made himself visible.

"John!"

The call came from far off, and was almost drowned out by the thunder and rain. When it was repeated, he homed in on it and started walking. Before he got ten yards into a wooded area, Abigail rushed out and threw her arms around him. Her sudden hug almost knocked him over, but he spun her about and kept his balance.

"John, John, it's so terrible! He's gone crazy."

"Did he kill Quinton?"

"He knew. Quinton knew. That's why William shot him."

"The servant knew Cheswick had killed his brother?"

Abigail bobbed her head up and down in agreement, sobbing harder now.

"You saw Pete—your brother—in the coffin and knew what had happened? Isn't that right?"

"He's a crack shot, John. William can take out the eye of a pigeon at a hundred paces. I didn't know why he wanted to go to the mine, but he knew Percival was driving freight there."

"The letter he had," Slocum said, remembering the folded page Cheswick had tucked away. "Someone found Pete for him, and he was hunting him down."

"We went all around Virginia City, but I didn't realize he was looking for Percival. Oh, John, what am I going to do?"

"Maybe you won't have to do anything," he said. She looked up at him, her blue eyes blazing. "There's a Scotland Yard detective with your brother right now. He suspects William killed Percival, and maybe even Ralph as well."

"Ralph deserved whatever he got," she said with acid-laced words. "He was a bounder and a knave."

"If you go back now, your brother's likely to start shooting. I think Partridge can handle him, if he doesn't get too violent."

"Partridge? The Scotland Yard policeman?"

"You know him?"

"He's had a vendetta against the Cheswick family for years. All save Ralph. They were like two peas in a pod."

Slocum considered this. He frowned as he turned over all the jagged pieces in his head, trying to put everything together into a picture that made sense.

Abigail distracted him by kissing him hard on the lips. With the rain pouring down around them, all Slocum could do was return the kiss and feel her warm body crushed against his. They turned slowly, the kiss deepening until Abigail broke off, gasping for breath.

"You are too much of a man for me. More than—" She abruptly cut off her sentence, then flashed him her wicked smile.

"More than who?" Slocum said.

"You wouldn't want to know." Abigail began unfastening her blouse and peeling the soaked fabric from her body. It came free like a snake shedding its skin until her firm, high breasts were wantonly exposed. Capping each was the brownish, hard nubbin of a nipple. Slocum bent over as she arched her back, offering them to him. His lips touched one. She gasped out in delight. He suckled, then went to the other and repeated the oral assault. Abigail's knees gave way under her, forcing Slocum to follow her to the wet ground.

He continued to lavish kisses on her breasts until she was writhing about under him. He pulled back and looked into her passion-racked face.

"More than who?" he repeated.

"Quinton," she sobbed out. "I was bedding a servant."

"Is that why your brother killed him?"

"John, please, this isn't the time. I want you so badly. I *need* you!" She rocked back on the wet bed of leaves and pine needles, and lifted her knees until her feet were flat on the ground. She began pulling up her skirt, inch by inch, revealing her shining, wet legs. Then he saw more than her calves or knees or thighs. Nestled between was a fleecy mat that beckoned to him.

He dropped his gun belt as he continued to stare at her. A tiny smile danced on her lips. She lay back, eyes closed and about the most beautiful woman he had ever seen as the rain spattered off her snowy white flesh. Her breasts rose and fell as her passion grew. When she parted her legs for him and he moved between them, Slocum thought he was going to explode then and there.

Her trembling hand reached down and took him, guided him, drew him to the point where he could not control himself any more. He slid forward into her lust-slickened tightness. When he was fully within her, he gulped and tried to control his urges. She tensed her muscles around him and squeezed down lovingly.

"You're too much for me," he said.

"No, no, not yet, John. Not yet. I want so much from you!"

She clawed at his upper arms and pulled him forward. She kissed him fervently. Her tongue flickered out and danced across his. Then she fell back to the ground, panting.

He withdrew until only the head of his erection remained within her nether lips. He thrust forward smoothly and buried himself once more in her heated paradise. She lifted her knees and grabbed them, further tightening herself around his manhood.

Slocum felt his control slipping away and began thrusting more powerfully. He wanted as much from her as he could get. The rain on his back, the sight of her passion, the heat and moistness and way she clenched down hard on him every time he entered her all took its toll. Slocum let out an animal cry and began stroking like a steam locomotive. Harder, deeper, he moved, until the friction mounted to the point where he could no longer sustain himself. He groaned as he shot his seed.

Abigail rocked to and fro, bringing her knees up even more, and then a flush spread from her face all the way down to the tops of her breasts. She sobbed and then relaxed. Slocum melted within her as he stared at her lovely face.

"I've never had a lover as good as you," she said in a whisper he could barely hear over the rain hammering the leaves above their heads.

"You aren't going to be safe unless Partridge arrests your brother," he said. "He killed Quinton. And I think he also killed Pete."

"And don't forget Ralph," she said, sitting up and pushing down her skirt. Abigail began fastening her blouse again, but it was muddy and wet and refused to button properly. Slocum helped her, giving them both additional pleasure.

When he finally strapped on his six-gun, he had to find a dry shirttail to wipe off his Colt. The mechanism was sensitive to dirt and water, and he needed it to function perfectly when he returned to Cheswick's camp. If Partridge hadn't already arrested him, Slocum would push the matter forward—at gunpoint if necessary. This was the only way Abigail could be safe again.

"Be careful, John. William is a killer. I . . . I never thought he would do what he did to become a duke."

"That's a high position," Slocum said. "The estate must be worth a fortune."

"A king's ransom," she said. "Literally. That's how the Cheswick family became so powerful two hundred years ago. A much smaller castle was pledged as ransom for the king. They were rewarded well for their loyalty."

"Yeah," Slocum said. He knew men did crazy things for money and power. Killing his two older brothers hardly mattered when the reward was so great. That must have occurred to William Cheswick over a period of years. A man who could kill his own flesh and blood was not one to turn your back on.

Slocum and Abigail made their way through the forest. She clung to his arm and pressed her cheek into his shoulder until they came to the clearing where the tent flapped wildly in the wind.

"Go on, John. Go get him. Be careful. He's got a pistol."

"Something's wrong," Slocum said. Before, he had seen two shadows against the canvas. There weren't any now. "Stay here."

"I have to see!"

"Stay *here*," he said harshly. Slocum drew his six-shooter and went to the tent flap. He pushed it open and looked inside, but could not see much since the coal oil lamp had been extinguished.

A small noise from the center of the tent put him on guard.

He slipped around the tent flap and moved along the perimeter, his eyes slowly adjusting to the darkness. When a bolt of lighting momentarily illuminated everything, he rushed forward and knelt by Lionel Partridge's side. The Scotland Yard detective lay on the ground between the two chairs where he and Cheswick had sat.

"Partridge, are you all right?" Slocum lifted the man's head, and again noted how frail he seemed. Eyelids fluttered and finally opened.

"He's gone, Mr. Slocum. I gave away my hand. He guessed I was a detective and shot me before I could arrest him."

"Just rest," Slocum said. "We'll patch you up."

"Good," Partridge said, then slipped into unconsciousness. Slocum lowered his head, wondering how long the man had before he died of the gunshot wound in his chest, about the same spot where Quinton had been shot.

He guessed that it wasn't going to be long before he had to dig another grave.

18

"He's the detective? I never saw him before, only heard of him from Ralph." Abigail looked at Partridge lying on the floor, covered with a blanket and paler than death. She shook her head in wonder. "It's hard to believe he came all the way to this country to arrest Percival."

"That's what he said." Slocum dropped water onto Partridge's parched lips. The man stirred and weakly licked at the moisture. His eyes fluttered open, and he mouthed that he wanted more water. Slocum let him have a little bit from a cup. Partridge sighed, relaxed, and seemed to go to sleep.

"Is he dead?"

Slocum put his hand on Partridge's throat.

"He's alive. His pulse is mighty strong. A tough old bird."

"William is out there somewhere. Why'd he run?" she asked.

"I was gone. You were gone. He wants to do some more killing is my guess."

"I thought I knew him. I can't believe he might try to kill me."

"When a man gets the taste of blood, it's hard to get it out of his mouth," Slocum said. He had seen killers in his day who murdered for the sheer thrill of seeing a man die. One thing always happened. The thrill became less with every murder, until they had to do something more to get the same excitement. About this time, somebody caught up with them and they died.

He shrugged it off. Maybe that was what they sought in the first place. There wasn't anything more terrifying than facing your own death. When enough men had died at your hand, you had to wonder what it was that happened the instant after a bullet ripped through a heart or head and want it for yourself.

"What do we do?" she asked.

"Get some sleep," Slocum said. "The rain's not letting up."

"What about William?"

"He might be back. We can pitch camp somewhere else, if that worries you," Slocum said. "He'd track us down. I say, make our stand here. Moving Partridge might not be such a good idea, even if he seems all right now."

"He's got one foot over the doorway of death!"

Slocum had seen men who looked perfectly healthy die in the wink of an eye. Others, like Partridge, were puny specimens but it took a powerful lot to kill them.

"Go on, get some sleep," Slocum said. "I'll stand watch."

"Very well," Abigail said. "It'd be more fun if you . . . slept with me."

"Too dangerous," Slocum said. "You know that."

"Oh, very well. Be practical. But it's so romantic listening to the rain against the canvas while you make love."

"You and Quinton do that?" Slocum wasn't sure why he prodded her like that. Her eyes flashed angrily; then she spun and walked off, head high and defiant. He watched her as she found a blanket and pulled it around herself, making a point of not looking in his direction. In a few minutes, her head sagged forward and she snored softly.

Slocum went out into the rain and made a quick circuit of the camp, hunting for Cheswick. If the man lurked out in the darkness, he was hidden too well for Slocum to spot. Returning to the tent, he shook himself and got some water off, then sat in a chair and leaned back. It was more comfortable than he remembered. He began drifting off to sleep, and awoke with a start when sunlight slanted through the open tent flap. Slocum sat up and looked around. Abigail was still asleep, but Partridge was nowhere to be seen.

As he stood, a piece of paper fluttered to the ground. He snatched it up and quickly scanned it.

"Son of a bitch," Slocum said. He'd started to leave when Abigail called out to him.

"John, what's wrong?"

"Partridge went after your brother."

"What? He was dead. Almost dead. How could he?"

"The man's got more sand in his gizzard than's good for him. I'll find him." Slocum waited for Abigail to protest. He wasn't too surprised when she didn't.

"Be careful," she said. "William is a marksman. With his elephant rifle, he can hit a silver dollar at a hundred yards."

"About as good as the shot he made killing his own brother," Slocum said. He took a quick look around, damning himself for not noticing earlier. Cheswick's rifle was gone from its case. The Brit was doubly dangerous now. All he needed to do was sit off a few hundred yards and wait for his prey to get clear. Slocum had heard that a bullet shot from a long distance could kill before the sound reached the victim. He had noticed that the sound trailed when he had been shot at, but had no idea how big a difference there was in the time between a rifle's report and death, or why this was true.

Staying out of range was probably impossible. He had to

be more clever—and hope he found Lionel Partridge before the detective blundered into Cheswick's sights.

He mounted and rode around the campsite, using the elevation to look for tracks. The rain had been fierce, but some indentations in the ground provided Slocum with his only spoor. He followed a ways, and finally got a clear hoofprint. Partridge had ridden out just as the rain stopped. The mud didn't hold tracks well, but now and then the detective rode over a rockier section and gave Slocum a hint as to his direction from a bright, new scratch made by a horseshoe against stone.

It was a direction Slocum didn't much like. Partridge was headed for the mountain peaks back in the direction of Virginia City. Whether by instinct or because he knew how William Cheswick thought, the Scotland Yard detective unerringly rode for a pass that would take him over the mountains and back to the boomtown.

At midday, Slocum took a break. He watered his mare and cleaned both his Colt Navy and his Winchester. The rifle balanced nicely in his hand and he brought it to his shoulder, sighting along the barrel. He could hit a deer at a hundred yards, but hitting a man at three times that would be more luck than skill. He lowered the rifle and wondered if that was what Cheswick had in mind. Sit, wait, shoot?

He ate a quick, cold meal and then pressed on. Partridge's tracks were more distinct now as the sun beat down on the meadowland and dried the soil. Although it was more a guess than sure knowledge, Slocum thought the detective was only about an hour ahead of him. If Slocum had ridden directly, trusting that Partridge wasn't veering from the road through the pass, he would have overtaken him by now. But missing a sudden deviation from the track would have meant lost time and probably Partridge's death. Slocum preferred to be sure.

Then he knew he was on the trail. A powerful rifle fired in the distance ahead. Slocum stood in the stirrups and looked around for William Cheswick, but did not see him. The bull-throated report could only have come from the man's elephant rifle. Slocum touched the empty shell casing in his pocket. It had saved him from the Paiutes and was his lucky charm now.

"Let's go find some of your brass relatives," Slocum said softly as he felt the outline of the cartridge in his vest pocket. A second report echoed through the meadow. Cheswick had missed with his first shot. Was his second any better? Slocum knew galloping to find out might make a third shot successful, but if he didn't hurry, Partridge might die.

Slocum tried to convince himself that Partridge wasn't dead yet. The man had luck on his side. How Cheswick had shot him in the chest and he had not only lived, but recovered enough to ride after his quarry, was beyond Slocum. Determined men always amazed him.

He came to the edge of a forest and looked down a long, rocky trail that joined a road through the mountain pass a mile to the west. From the size of the ruts and how the weeds were freshly crushed in spite of the rain, this had to be a road leading into Virginia City. Partridge's instinct about where Cheswick would run had proved accurate.

Slocum only hoped Cheswick's marksmanship wasn't as good as the detective's skills.

He took the field glasses from his saddlebags and slowly scanned the terrain. He found Partridge quickly enough. The detective cowered behind a large boulder a hundred yards down the slope. How he hunkered behind the rock gave Slocum an idea where to hunt for Cheswick. He swung the binoculars around and studied the mouth to a canyon leading away at an angle. At first he saw nothing. Then he caught a silver flash as sunlight reflected off the sighting bead at the front of the large rifle.

"Mr. Slocum," shouted Partridge. "Be careful. He is up high."

"I've got him spotted, but he's more than four hundred yards away. There's nothing I can do," Slocum called back.

The instant the words left his mouth, his hat went flying. He grabbed for it and dropped it on the string around his neck. A new bullet hole had mysteriously appeared in the brim. A full second after the impact, he heard the rifle report.

Knowing he was exposed, he wheeled his mare around and galloped for cover in the forest. A second round tore a limb from a nearby tree. Cheswick had missed him by several feet with that shot. Then Slocum was safely in the woods. He dismounted and cautiously made his way back to a spot where he could call down to Partridge.

"He'll pick you off eventually," Slocum shouted. "I'll draw his fire. Can you make it back uphill?"

"Are the woods any safer?"

"Your horse able to gallop back here?"

"I shall see," Partridge said with determination. He edged around the boulder. Slocum saw a geyser of rock and smoke appear on the top of the boulder, forcing Partridge to duck back. His horse stood some distance away. If Cheswick wanted to end this quickly, he would shoot Partridge's horse.

But where would be the sport in that? Slocum had begun to understand how the Brit thought. This was not murder, but grand adventure for him, and a chance to show how superior he was. It didn't matter that Partridge couldn't shoot back. A deer or buffalo couldn't either. The thrill came in the stalking and the accurate shot that brought down the prey.

A fleeting thought crossed Slocum's mind. Why had Cheswick shot Quinton the way he had? The burned spot on the servant's coat gave mute evidence that the pistol muzzle had been a foot or less away. There was no sport in killing a man that way. Or so it ought to seem from Cheswick's view. Slocum pushed that from his mind. Quinton might have insulted him or done something to anger his employer. The elephant gun trained alternately on Partridge and Slocum was the only thing that counted right now.

"Get ready," Slocum shouted.

He returned to the forest, patted his mare's neck, and said softly, "We'll flush him. Wait and see." He drew the Winchester from its saddle sheath, mounted, and then took a deep breath. "Giddyap!" His heels raked the mare's flanks and sent the valiant horse rocketing toward the mouth of the canyon.

Slocum remembered more than one frontal assault he had taken part in during the war. Those were different. The cavalry and soldiers were ordered to attack directly ahead of where they started. To veer to either side would bunch up troops, and probably invite a bullet in the back from the wave of his own soldiers attacking immediately behind. Slocum had no such orders now. He zigzagged as he rode, sometimes riding a long way only to cut back, and other times allowing his horse to go only a few strides before changing direction.

Cheswick might have been a good shot, but the rapid advance and even swifter changes in direction prevented him from drawing a bead with the large caliber rifle. When Slocum got closer, he swung up his own rifle and began firing in Cheswick's direction. Such shots hitting the sniper would be more luck than skill. Slocum bounced as his mare took the rocky ground the best she could, but his skills during the war had included attacks on towns while on horseback. He might not be able to shoot this way as good as an Indian, but he was good enough.

He saw Cheswick stand to take a shot. Slocum's bullet whanged off the rock directly in front of the Britisher and ricocheted past him, ruining his aim. This brought Slocum another dozen yards closer before Cheswick recovered.

"You're going to die, Slocum. Stop and let me make a clean shot!"

Slocum fired the best he could—and it was good enough to drive Cheswick behind the rock. If the elephant gun wasn't trained on him, it couldn't kill him. Slocum kept riding when he got to the mouth of the canyon, and raced past where Cheswick waited.

This was all he could hope for. Cheswick had no choice now but to come after Slocum and let Partridge go. If he tried to shoot the detective, he had to turn his back on Slocum. The murderer knew that mercy had long since died in Slocum's breast.

Putting his head down, Slocum rode on. By now, Partridge had escaped. It was time to remove William Cheswick permanently.

Slocum slowed, turned around, and started to gallop back to the canyon mouth. Two quick rounds aimed at him convinced him he had to go deeper into the canyon. This was dangerous because Cheswick had only to make one good shot and Slocum would be as dead as Percival Cheswick. He went back into the canyon, looking for a way out. He could always go after Cheswick later, after he rode out the other end of the canyon.

He drew rein and stared after he had ridden less than a quarter mile. He had ridden into a box canyon.

Trapped!

19

The canyon walls were almost vertical, rising more than fifty feet. Search as he might, Slocum couldn't find a trail to either rim. He realized it would be a trail to his death if he even tried, since Cheswick could see him moving and take his time with a single shot to bring him down. For all he knew, Cheswick had a tripod to rest his powerful rifle on, making his aim even steadier.

He rode all the way into the canyon, hoping to find a crevice that penetrated through the rock to another canyon and safety. If it existed, Slocum missed it. As desperate as he was becoming, he would have spotted any break in the shrubs growing out of solid rock or felt wind whistling through from a distance. The impossible closeness of the rock walls turned this canyon into a sweat lodge—or was it his increasing fear that Cheswick had him dead to rights?

Slocum refused to simply ride out and let the Brit shoot him. This was his country, and he could find a way of turning terrain to his benefit. If only he had time.

A shot boomed down the canyon and almost deafened him. Where the slug went, he didn't know. Cheswick was trying to flush him, make him think he had a bead on him. Slocum gentled his horse, then dismounted. He reloaded his rifle and began the slow sneak toward the mouth of the canyon where Cheswick waited for him. Staying close to one wall lowered the risk of being seen, but it also limited where he could run. All he needed to do was be sure Cheswick wasn't on the far side.

Another shot echoed. Slocum knew Cheswick did this to confuse him. He tried to locate the source of the report, but after it bounced off the rock walls a couple times, it sounded as if it came from everywhere all at once. Again, the slug went somewhere far from him.

Emboldened by the idea that Cheswick was shooting at movement elsewhere, perhaps an unfortunate coyote or timber wolf, Slocum moved quickly to get into range so he could take out his foe. Slocum had taken only a couple strides when he realized that Cheswick had laid a cunning trap for him. The man had shot down the canyon to lull him into thinking he had no idea where Slocum was.

Slocum bent his knees and kicked as hard as he could, and still barely missed getting the heavy-caliber slug in his body. A fiery track ran across his side and his inner left arm, showing how deadly accurate Cheswick was with his elephant gun. If Slocum hadn't dodged when he did, that bullet would have ripped out his heart. Slocum hit the ground hard, rolled, and winced as he picked up nettles from a patch of foxtail. The sharp spines were better than an ounce of lead in his chest, though, and he didn't stop moving until he was certain he was protected by heavy rock from Cheswick's accurate fire.

He winced as he tried to lift his left arm. The bullet had gouged out a shallow trough along his forearm, and then had taken some skin from his side with it before disappearing into the canyon. He tore strips from his shirt and patched himself up the best he could. Moving became painful, and lifting his left arm to hold the front guard on his rifle was a chore that would become increasingly onerous. He had to kill Cheswick fast or he would be the victim.

Once he had tied the cloth strips around his chest in a crude bandage and taken care of his arm to stanch the oozing blood, he waited for Cheswick to taunt him. The man's immense arrogance would make him call out his threats, his cries of superiority, and that would let Slocum find him. But Cheswick proved too smart a hunter to reveal his position with such juvenile goading. All Slocum heard was the stillness all around.

He wondered if this was what a grave was like once one was inside it.

The heat became oppressive, and the silence rubbed his nerves raw. His wounds began to itch and then hurt, as if his arm and ribs had been dipped in fire. He stayed still, every sense alert for Cheswick to betray himself.

After ten minutes, Slocum began to despair. Cheswick knew he hadn't made a killing shot, but was not anxious to track down his prey. If the Britisher remained hidden, he held the upper hand. Slocum could never sneak past him out of this narrow-mouthed canyon, and even if he did, then what? Slocum had left his horse at the far end of the box canyon. It was a long walk anywhere in this part of Nevada. Worse, the nearest town wasn't likely to welcome him with open arms. More likely, the marshal and citizens of Virginia City would string him up without ever listening to his story.

Still, the only plan he had was getting past Cheswick and turning the tables. Trap the killer in the canyon. Then he could play with him like Cheswick was toying with him now. Slocum chanced a quick look around the edge of the rock giving him dubious sanctuary, hoping to spot the sniper. He saw small movement fifteen feet up the side of the far canyon wall, but it might have been fitful wind rustling the leaves of a bush.

Or it might be Cheswick.

Slocum decided that the time was ripe for him to attack. He positioned his rifle carefully, steadying it on the rock. He didn't have to worry about windage in the still air of the canyon. Then he drew back on the trigger. Long years of practice with this rifle gave him the drop and distance corrections without even thinking about them. His bullet ripped through the bush he had seen fluttering about.

Nothing.

The waiting game lengthened into minutes when neither of the snipers took the initiative. Slocum began to think Cheswick might have left, but there was no reason to abandon his quarry like that when he held the winning hand by commanding the canyon mouth. The notion that Cheswick was an even better hunter than Slocum began to worry at him like the nettles still in his legs and arms. If Slocum hadn't fired that last round, Cheswick might wonder if his enemy was dead or so seriously wounded he could never fight back. With the shot, Slocum knew now that he had lost what slim advantage he'd had.

This fight would be determined by whoever got the first, best target. Cheswick knew Slocum was still alive and fighting. Slocum had to guess that Cheswick was still in the battle.

Slocum looked at the sky, wishing the storm would build and come in with a vengeance again so he could escape under its watery cover. Only blue sky arched above the canyon walls. Nightfall could give him the same advantage. Slocum could move like an Apache, but he knew twilight might be too far off to do him any good. His wounds seeped blood and pus and did not clot over. Simply standing sapped energy from him.

The only thing he could do was launch a frontal attack and hope Cheswick showed himself. As he ran, Slocum tried to dodge, but found his movements slow and jerky. This saved his life when he moved left and tried to dodge in the other direction, only to find that his legs refused to respond. If he had gone the direction he tried, a bullet would have ended his life. As it was, Cheswick's round whined past and tore off a splinter of rock that nicked Slocum's good arm. He fell forward and wiggled like a snake behind a bush. This afforded little cover and no protection, so he kept moving.

Another of the heavy rounds from the elephant gun ripped apart the bush where he had lain for only a few seconds.

Slocum had less cover here, but enough for him to swing his rifle around, get an idea where Cheswick had to be hiding, and fire a few rounds in that direction. A smile came to his lips.

"Got you, you son of a bitch."

Slocum triggered off another round into the spot where Cheswick had to be hiding. From the sudden movement behind the brush, he knew he had winged the Brit. But how seriously had he wounded him? The only way to find out was to stand and make his way across an open stretch.

"Three aces," Slocum said softly. His luck had been terrible so far. In his gut, he knew that he wouldn't make it, so he remained still, playing a waiting game.

Cheswick let out a loud cry and thrashed through the brush, coming fully into Slocum's view. Not caring why Cheswick revealed himself so carelessly, Slocum fired and fired again. His rifle came up empty, or he would have fired one more killing shot.

Cheswick thrashed about on the ground and tried to stand. He couldn't. One of Slocum's bullets had caught him in the leg. He tumbled down a rocky slope and screamed at the top of his lungs.

Without hesitation now, Slocum drew his six-shooter and ran as hard as he could to get within range. By the time he had a clear shot, he saw that it wouldn't be needed. Lionel Partridge came through the brush where Cheswick had hidden and aimed his rifle directly at the fallen murderer.

Caught between Slocum and Partridge, Cheswick threw up his hands and surrendered. It took all of Slocum's willpower not to simply gun the man down. He looked up at the Scotland Yard detective, and saw the same decision being made.

"You got him, Partridge. Take him back to stand trial," Slocum shouted.

"I rather don't like people telling me such things, Mr. Slocum—especially when they are right."

Both advanced on their prisoner.

"You're nothing but a back-shooting snake," Slocum said, "and it'll be good knowing you'll go to the gallows for at least one murder."

"One?" Cheswick laughed maniacally. "One! The very one I'll be tried for I didn't commit!"

"What's he mean?" Slocum asked Partridge, who had slipped and slid down the slope to join them.

"It is as I suspected. His wife's the culprit who poisoned Ralph Cheswick."

"His wife?" Slocum looked hard at Cheswick, then at Partridge for an explanation.

"You know her. His wife, Abigail Cheswick."

20

"The bitch tried to kill me," William Cheswick said with venom. "If it hadn't been for Quinton, I'd be dead."

"What do you mean?" Slocum circled and stood beside Partridge to face Cheswick. The look of pure hatred on Cheswick's aristocratic face turned him into a vicious animal.

"I didn't kill Quinton. He was my servant. He gave his life to save me when she tried to kill me."

"But you shot your brother," Slocum said.

"Percival? He was a fool," Cheswick said. "Abigail poisoned Ralph and we came to this horrid place to remove Percival before he found out he was the new duke." He took a deep breath and then sneered. "It wasn't enough for her to share my wealth. She wanted it all."

"I don't understand. Women can't inherit."

"You refer to the law of primogeniture, old chap," Partridge said. "While it is true his wife was not in the line of ascension for a royal title, the laws of England allow a wife a large share of an estate should her husband die."

"She wouldn't be a duchess but she'd own the estate?"

182

"And a considerable portfolio of stocks in very valuable companies in London and Paris, not to mention the jewelry," said Cheswick. "Oh, yes, dear Abigail wanted it all, and I was becoming a nuisance."

"You mean you were going to trade her in for a younger woman," Partridge said. "I heard the rumors. Speaking with Miss Simpson-Jones put me on your trail to the Colonies," Partridge said. "No one knew where Percival had gone, but you must have learned his whereabouts."

"He got a letter," Slocum said.

"A former Pinkerton agent," Cheswick said, "willing to collect a few extra pennies for his work proved quite the detective."

"So you're only guilty of shooting your brother Percival?" Slocum scratched his chin when he saw Cheswick's reaction. There was something the man was not telling. Slocum looked at Partridge for confirmation.

"Only Percival," the detective said, "and his wife did in both Ralph and Quinton. Oh, she will answer for that. We do not hang women in England, but she will be in prison for a jolly long time. This one, though," he said, pointing his rifle at Cheswick, "this one will be hanged."

Partridge motioned for his prisoner to move. Cheswick hobbled along, injured far worse by Slocum's bullet than his slug had wounded Slocum. As they walked from the narrow canyon, Slocum thought hard on everything Cheswick had said. There was more, but he didn't know what it might be.

"Thanks for diverting him," Slocum said. "If you hadn't flushed him when you did, he would have killed me for certain." He bent, picked up the fallen elephant rifle, and opened the breech. Both rounds were expended. Slocum reached into his pocket and drew out the shell casing that had saved him from the Paiutes. He popped both the spent cartridges out and tucked them into his vest pocket with the first one.

"A bit of superstition, eh?" Partridge asked.

"Something like that." Slocum made no move to help their prisoner when Cheswick began slowing and finally stumbled and fell to the ground. His leg had given way under him. Partridge was more charitable and helped Cheswick bandage the wound.

"Must keep him alive until we return to the Old Bailey for trial."

Slocum only nodded, not sure what Partridge meant. The details of the confession still bothered him. Cheswick was a murderer, but Abigail—his wife!—was doubly so.

"Why'd she get me out of jail in Virginia City?" Slocum asked. "And she got me out of the shed when the Climax foreman locked me up. Why not let me take the fall for your murders?"

Even as the words slipped from his lips, Slocum knew what had happened.

"She got me out of the Virginia City jail to throw off the posse," Slocum said suddenly. "*You* killed Renfro, and she didn't want anyone on your trail interfering until you had killed Percival."

"You have a remarkably clever mind, Slocum," Cheswick said. "I had never killed anyone and wanted to know that I could do it. Renfro was convenient, that's all."

"You killed and robbed him!"

"I certainly didn't need the money. That smeary scrip you call greenbacks is hardly money to me. Real money is a pound note with Queen Victoria's likeness on it."

"But he took it," Partridge said. He fished in a coat pocket and pulled out a wad of greenbacks. "I searched his luggage and found this."

"Proving it came from Renfro's dead body's not possible," Slocum said.

"It came from his pocket," Cheswick said. "I killed him—and it felt good. I knew then that I could kill my own brother." Cheswick made a gun out of his index finger and thumb and sighted down it, then laughed. "I only wish I had been armed when dear Abigail tried to kill me."

"This is one hell of a family," Slocum said.

"You enjoy her, Slocum? Did she beguile you with her charms?"

"Why did you go along with her posing as your sister?" Slocum asked. Cheswick had to know what his wife was doing.

"She always had a mind of her own, and truthfully, you wouldn't be her first dalliance." Cheswick laughed. "I certainly had mine."

"Miss Simpson-Jones," Partridge said.

"She was the most recent," Cheswick said. "How I wish Abigail knew of her."

"You'll get the chance to tell her," Slocum said. He whistled and waited for his mare to come trotting up. Less than an hour later, the trio rode back into the camp. The red, white, and blue tent flapped fitfully in the wind, looking as if huge lungs gasped for breath.

"Watch him," Slocum said told Partridge. He saw that the detective had his pistol covering Cheswick. Slocum stepped down from his mare and went to the tent flap. He pushed it back and peered inside.

Abigail looked up, startled. The confusion crossed her face, then she smiled. He saw it for the insincere warmth that it was.

"John, darling. I was just going through William's things, looking for—" She looked hard at him. "What's wrong, John?"

"What would you say if I told you he was dead?"

"William? Dead?" The sun came out on her face, and then she tried to hide her elation. "Tell me it's not so!"

She came to him.

"It's not true," Slocum said. "Partridge captured him and has him prisoner." Slocum felt a small touch of satisfaction when he saw her expression change again, this time to one of horror. "You killed Ralph and you shot Quinton," he said.

"I never killed Quinton! William did that! He tried to shoot me and Quinton got between us!"

She came for him, her hand flashing from the folds of her skirt. A derringer gleamed in the dim light. Before she could aim, Slocum caught her wrist and forced her to drop it.

"You're going to stand trial for killing Ralph Cheswick," he said. "Nobody might prove you killed Quinton, but that hardly matters."

"You miserable worm. You—"

Abigail began sputtering with curses. Slocum pulled her to him and kissed her suddenly, flustering her. She stared up at him when he broke off the kiss.

"Why'd you do that?" she asked.

"I wanted to make sure I wasn't going to miss you."

"Thanks," Slocum said, shaking Lionel Partridge's hand. "You got me out of a world of trouble."

"It took your silver tongue to convince that barman to allow me to take them both back to England," the detective said. He looked toward the stagecoach depot where William and Abigail Cheswick were chained together. They sat half turned in different directions, pointedly ignoring each other. Marshal Dinks and Mac had listened in amazement as Abigail and William blamed each other for every crime under the sun—but the only ones that Slocum cared about were the deaths of Renfro and Pete. Mac was slower to come around, but he finally grudgingly admitted the evidence against Slocum didn't amount to a hill of beans.

"There's my ride to San Francisco," Partridge said, seeing the Wells Fargo stage come rattling up.

"It's a long way back to England. Don't let them gull you," Slocum said.

"No more than an Indian cobra can beguile me. I know how dangerous both of them are," Partridge said.

Slocum left the detective busily shifting locks and chains, getting his prisoners secured in the stagecoach. William Cheswick wouldn't look at Slocum, but Abigail stared daggers at him. As the stage rattled off, heading for the coast, he was glad to see the last of them.

He patted the wad of money in his pocket. There hadn't been any reason to tell the marshal that this was the poke Renfro had been carrying when Cheswick murdered him. For all he had been through, Slocum felt he was owed. Partridge had agreed.

Slocum walked toward the Mountain of Gold Saloon, then decided he would not be welcome there, even if Mac had reluctantly admitted he was innocent. His steps took him farther down the street to the larger Bucket of Blood. The floor was ankle deep in sawdust, and several poker games were already in progress, although it was only eight in the morning.

Finding an empty chair, Slocum sat down and was dealt in the next hand. He looked around the table and saw two miners, a cowboy, and a man who might have been a tinker or a professional gambler.

"What's yer bet, mister?" the tinker asked.

Slocum picked up his cards and scanned them.

Three aces.

"I fold," he said, pushing back from the table. It was too late to catch a ride on the stage with Partridge, but it wasn't too late for him to hit the trail to somewhere else, as long as it was far, far away from Virginia City.